Samuel Eberly Gross

The Merchant Prince of Cornville

A Comedy

Samuel Eberly Gross

The Merchant Prince of Cornville
A Comedy

ISBN/EAN: 9783744788397

Printed in Europe, USA, Canada, Australia, Japan

Cover: Foto ©Andreas Hilbeck / pixelio.de

More available books at **www.hansebooks.com**

The

Merchant Prince of Cornville

A COMEDY

BY SAMUEL EBERLY GROSS

Represented in London, England, at the Novelty Theatre, on November 11, 1896.

CHICAGO AND NEW YORK
RAND, McNALLY & COMPANY,
PUBLISHERS.

The Merchant Prince of Cornville

A COMEDY

The Merchant Prince of Cornville.

A Comedy.

THE CHARACTERS.

WHETSTONE	The Merchant Prince, suitor to Violet.
BLUEGRASS	His secretary.
SCYTHE	A scientist.
IDEAL	A poet, suitor to Violet.
NORTHLAKE	A philosopher.
FOPDOODLE	A fop, suitor to Violet.
TOM	His valet.
PUNCH	A miscellaneous person.
JACK	Son to Northlake and Catharine.
POMPEY	A butler.
HANNIBAL	A servant.
VIOLET	Niece and ward to Northlake.
NINON	Her maid.
CATHARINE	Former wife to Northlake.
SUSAN	Housekeeper to Whetstone.

Maskers, Musicians, etc.

PLACE . . . The Seaside.

TIME . . . The Last Quarter of the Nineteenth Century.

SYNOPSIS OF SCENERY AND INCIDENTS.

ACT I.

SCENE I. *An orchard by the sea. Sunrise. The pursuit and discovery.*

II. *A pavilion, with view of the sea. The arrival of the Merchant Prince.*

ACT II.

SCENE I. *On the seashore. Business, science, and romance.*

II. *Portico of the Dolphin Inn. A speculation in love.*

III. *A costumer's shop. A study in characters.*

IV. *A street. The fop and the ape.*

V. *A boudoir. Before the masquerade.*

ACT III.

SCENE I. *A masquerade. Assembly of the maskers.*

II. *A balcony. The lover in armor.*

III. *The same. A minor love affair.*

IV. *The same. Hearts unmasked.*

ACT IV.

SCENE I. *A room at the Dolphin Inn. The hour before the combat.*

II. *A clearing in a wood. The literary duel.*

III. *The Glen of Ferns. Love's high noon.*

ACT V.

SCENE I. *A room at the Dolphin Inn. A prelude to a serenade.*

II. *A hall in a villa. A speculation in stocks.*

III. *A lawn before a villa. The serenade and finale.*

The Merchant Prince of Cornville.

A COMEDY.

Act the First.

Enter IDEAL.

IDEAL.

The hour of dawn ! — how thrilling and intense !
The matin songs of birds, that dart and soar
On quivering wings, now break upon the sense
As sharply as the cannon's voice at mid-day ;
In yonder wood that guards the sea-cliff's wall,
Where sullen shadows shrink away and flee
Before the rising sun's advancing spears,
The day-detesting owl hath turned his back
Unto the light, and sought the sheltering cowl
Of ivy web about the oak-tree thrown;
And all the glowing world, — wood, sea, and sky, —
Is most sublimely beautiful beneath
This pendulous light, that, like an avalanche
Of golden beams . . . But I have spoken the word
That halts my fancy's flight, and brings me back
To earth and its dull cares, and our dull age, —

The Merchant Prince

Our golden age 't is called : our age of gold,
Hard and material, when our best ideals
But folly seem, all things are bought and sold,
And even love itself is merchandise.
Alas ! the many years that I have known,
And many ills, in this same golden age,
Have brought their bitter harvest to my breast,
Like frozen grain beaten by winds unkind
From out the icy north ; but as those seeds
Fall sterile on the earth, nor glow with life,
So shall my sorrows take no living root
Within my bosom. . . . Now do I recall,
Like a sweet picture in a gallery hung,
How I last eve at early twilight watched
The figure of a lovely maiden bending
Tenderly o'er a vase of new-blown flowers,
Upon a breezy terrace, underneath
A green-hued lattice-work, that, like a shield
Embossed with morning-glories, hides and guards
Her chamber window.   Passing there this morn,
I looked upon the flowers as one might
Who, barred from out the walls of Paradise,
Would seize some blossom growing sweetly there ;
Then, while my eager heart tumultuous beat,
Sending the tell-tale blushes to my cheek,
I plucked a flower — this crimson, perfumed pink.
'T is woven from a clod of earth, and yet
To me 't is fairer than a star of heaven.
Sweet flower ! sweet flower ! last evening I did see

Thy mistress from her chamber casement lean
And gaze ecstatic on the pilgrim moon
Tracing a silvery path along the sky ;
But thou didst woo her from that magic gaze,
Drawing her to thee with the subtler force
Of finer particles than live within
The cold moon's slanting beams. . . .
But soft ! yonder my lady's self appears,
Slow moving down the orchard path.   I 'll seek
A covert by this tree.   Seeing the hunter
Doth fright the deer away.

[He hides behind an orchard tree.

Enter VIOLET.

VIOLET.

Which way 's the robber gone ? I 'm sure I saw him here.

IDEAL [*aside*].

What ! I 'm a robber, am I ?   Well, this tree hath no tell-
tale bark, and I 'll stay here.

VIOLET.

I thought I heard some one speak, but not from under-
ground, for he 's not a goblin ; nor yet from the sky, for
he 's not an angel ; nor yet from the earth, for no dreadful
man is near. Why, what is that in the sky ? 'T is last eve's
moon, that will not to her couch by day. To rest ! pale
planet.   O gentle moon, where is thy blush ?   Thou art

dismantled by the roseate sun.   Alack! what divine dramas are there in the skies!

> Oh, would that I within thy circlet's rim
> Might glide by curves of brightening lawns.   In thee
> The day is half a month till noon, and thoughts
> Are gentle as the velvet fawns that glide
> From out thy rustling groves.   In thee, rare flowers
> Their fragrant balms distil, and perfume wreathes
> The girdling hours.   Let me fancy this!

IDEAL.

Now doth she see her fragile fancies rise on wings of gossamer, like one who chases golden butterflies, flying before the dawn.   What sweet mysterious alchemy could beauty such as hers persuade!

VIOLET.

But list; what's this?   A spirit in the tree, — a talking spirit, too!   I'll listen; 'tis my privilege in this orchard. Go on, sweet spirit, I'm listening.   [*Pauses.*]   Nay, go on, my time is brief; or if thou 'dst rather, I'll not overhear.

IDEAL.

Nay, hear, sweet maid; I'm fated in this tree to dwell, and ne'er before so spoke my heart unto a maid.

VIOLET.

Canst thou not speak in rhymes?   Why, spirits should

be poets too; or is the tree's rind too hard? I do pity thee for a poor spirit.

IDEAL.

Nay, hear me. When the tree is in its blossom, then rhymes come fleetest; when the tree is in its fruitage, then rhymes come sweetest. Thou once, on such a time, didst sit beneath these ripening boughs, in sweetest reverie wrapt, and I, while musing on thy beauty and the gentle spirit within thee, didst weave these rhymes.

VIOLET.

I well remember it; and if thou art a truthful spirit I will listen to thy rhymes. Thou mayst begin.

IDEAL.

What pure mysterious alchemy
   Doth beauty chaste as thine persuade
To sublimate its crude degree
   In sweetest herbs of earth displayed!

VIOLET.

Stop, stop; I command thee! Thou art much too philo-sophical for a poet. I'm weary.

IDEAL.

Thou didst halt me in the middle of my verse.
   For I philosophy discern
      In quivering lips, in liquid eyes,
   In rounded neck, and cheeks that burn
      Like rose-leaves 'neath the radiant skies;

13

In hair as golden as the sun
  That wreathes the circling grove, and seems
As fine and delicately spun
  As if 't were woven of his beams.

Violet.

Thou 'rt much too flattering for a spirit. Thou art not
a cold spirit, but a warm one. Good spirits should be cold.
Mend thy rhymes, or I will leave thee in thy prison.

Ideal [aside].
I 'll learn if she beheld my robbery this morn.

[Aloud.] Didst thou awake?
    Didst thou awake?
That hour when moonbeams glide away
'Neath limpid tints of twinkling day,
When from the wires of its cage,
  That string between from bar to bar,
Thy prisoned bird, in tuneful rage,
  Awoke unto the morning star,
And sang unto the woodland wild
  That hides the sun beyond the hills,
And hides, in wavy foliage isled,
  The breezy nest of cooing bills?
    Didst thou awake?
    Didst thou awake?

Violet.

Why, that sounds like a morning serenade. Now indeed

do I know thee for a spirit of light-tripping gayety; but I'll answer no questions. I was wakened by a robber who from my chamber-window plucked my favorite flower. Spirits should know all things, and not be so inquisitive for ladies' secrets.

IDEAL.

Give me the wings of yonder lark,
 Soaring into the perfumed dawn,
Beyond the chimney's beckoning spark
 That, blackening, strews the beaten lawn.

For I, within this tree immured,
 With fervent glances scan the ships
That sail and sail until, obscured,
 The ivory fleet the ocean dips;

While swarms of white-winged memories,
 Like missive-bearing doves, arise
From out the pure pellucid seas,
 And float above these orchard skies.

VIOLET.

Why, what pretty fruit that tree doth bear! I have a mind, but, alas! not the heart, to leave thee in thy tree, to rhyme to me some other day. Art done? No answer. Then I'll rhyme, too. Spirit, thy art's infectious.

Move slow, thou circlet of the moon,
 Turn not to zones thy brightening lawns;
Let day be half a month till noon;
 Wake not with light thy distant dawns.

But, fie, why doth the genial sun make the moon so pale? I would not turn so pale were a man to appear in this orchard.

[*Pauses.*] Sweet spirit, appear, appear! No answer. Hast lost thy speech, or doth the tree's bark encompass thee too closely? If thou art in the trunk of this fair tree, I'll petition it with ardent lips to ope its close-bound rind and let thee out; but how? The tree cannot hear, being deaf, but the tree can feel, being alive; so then, I'll kiss thee, thou hard, hard tree. [*Bends to kiss the tree, when* IDEAL *appears and kisses her.*] What spirit art thou in man's disguise to thus affright a lady who ne'er did harm to thee, but wished thee well? How couldst thou treat me so?

IDEAL.

Fair maid, thou fill'st me with such keen delight I know not what to say, but pause for utterance, my lips being newly laden with a sweet burden.

VIOLET.

Nay, not so. Thou art too literal. I do entreat thee for an answer.

IDEAL.

Thou art the most fair complainant that e'er did sue for answer, and in a just cause, too. How could the earth resist the sun? How could the sea resist the tide? How could a spirit resist heaven?

VIOLET.

I thought thou wert a spirit who'd been in heaven long ago.

IDEAL.

Never before did I even dream of heaven; and for material answer make I this: Our spirits were kindred, and by that fair relationship I did salute thee so.

VIOLET.

Now do I know thee : thou art no spirit, but a robber, — a substantial robber who plucked my favorite pink from my window ; but I, rising in quick haste, followed thee adown this orchard path. Thou thought'st thou hadst escaped me. I did see thee but half plainly, by the dawn's most timorous light that through the lattice wooed my pillow.

IDEAL.

As thou didst wake ! Oh, would I were the dawn's most delicate light that wooed thy soul's fair stars exiled within thy crescent-curtained eyes !

VIOLET.

And if thou wert, thou wert but a robber still. Thou hast the flower in thy hand !

IDEAL.

Oh, I have treasured it ; yet will I return to thee the pink. 'Tis thy property.

VIOLET.

Nay, keep the flower, if thou lovest it so.

IDEAL.

Ay, then I 'll think it had its birth 'neath twilight's violet sky.

VIOLET.

Think not too lightly of the flower ; 't is most rare, — grown from a seed found in the tomb of an Egyptian mummy. She was an ancient princess who died in the flower of her youth from love ill requited: so read the antique parchment entombed with her,—a legend pitiful and true; but then, 't was three thousand years ago.

IDEAL.

Love has grown more constant since then.

VIOLET.

I hope thou wouldst not jest at love?

IDEAL.

Nay, not I. I'd sooner jest at all fair properties in heaven and earth than jest at love.

VIOLET.

'Tis a flower of ancient lineage. I planted it with mine own hands, and watched it grow. What joy I felt to see it grow, I ne'er can tell. When first its tender bud beseeched the sky, it was athirst; I brought it water from a crystal spring. From simple bud to leafy stalk it grew, and then the petals formed, giving sweet promise of a flower; till yesternight from its green husk the perfect blossom bloomed, and I did shed a tear upon it, thinking of that poor princess.

IDEAL.

Dost think her spirit lives in heaven?

VIOLET.

That do I most truly. I would not that thou thought'st differently. Thou couldst not be so cruel!

IDEAL.

Thy simple story moves me beyond the power of prayer. Now that the flower buried with her doth live, let it bequeath a legacy of love most true and constant to our hearts; so shall the princess from beyond see within our lives a perfect love wrought by her most heavenly agency. And here [*kneeling*], on bended knee, by thy dear hand that's clasped in mine, I vow, by all the subtle bonds that nature placed within the world to bind us to the truth, to love thee ever.

VIOLET.

Rise; thou art the planet of my maiden firmament. I do believe thee. My vow is linked with thine most sweetly and inseparably.

IDEAL.

Thy words are bright flowers, whose subtle sweets I do extract and hide away. Ay, I shall live on them when thou art absent, as the patient bee lives on his hoarded store in winter.

VIOLET.

I hope thou speakest truly as thou dost fairly, for thou speakest as a poet doth, and I have heard,—but pardon me; I'll not quote the idle gossip.

IDEAL.

I pray thee, do.

Violet.

Well, then, to heed thy prayer. I 've heard it rumored that poets, in their grammar, all the moods of love do conjugate in swift succession.

Ideal.

I 'll prove to thee that gossip is untrue.

Violet.

I 've heard that they are variable ; that they contract the four seasons into the compass of a day, — call the morning spring, the forenoon summer, the afternoon autumn, and the evening oft the depth of winter; that they in idle ways say thus: Why, prithee, this forenoon, being in love beneath the equator, I felt the fervent sun impart his fever to the earth ; but to-night, alack ! being out of love, Lapland hath no denizen colder than I. I pray thou wilt not treat me so.

Ideal.

By Heaven, 't is a scandal ! I 'd have thee try me. Use pique, jest, coldness, stratagem, and all the dire weapons in a maid's armory to try her lover, and if, knowing thou art true, I do not in all love's humors love thee still, why then —

Violet.

Yes, why then —

Ideal.

Why, then, I 'll return to dust.

VIOLET.

Alack! that would be unkind.

IDEAL.

Nay, try me.

VIOLET.

Perchance I may. [*Aside*] But only for a moment. [*Aloud*] How high's the sun, pray?

IDEAL [*looking at his watch*].

I'll be precise, and timely guard my answer. 'Tis nigh unto five o'clock; the minute-hand lacks one, the second-hand —

VIOLET.

Stop, stop! thou outspeedest Time himself. How desperately thou rushest from the hour to the minute hand — from thence there is but a fraction of time to the second hand, which I take to be not a good token; for thou hadst but a minute ago my hand, and yet thus swiftly thou wouldst approach a second hand.

IDEAL.

Shall we have no watches with second hands?

VIOLET.

I'll have no merchandising. Thou a poet and a lover, and lookest at thy watch to tell the sun's height! Alas! put up thy watch; lovers do not time themselves by watches. Thou wouldst not so at night register the moon's

21

height; but upon a pressing question, How high's the moon? wouldst answer, A little higher than yonder rose-bush, if the moon rose late; or, perchance, A little higher than yonder tree-top, if the moon rose early. The sun's as fine to me by day as the moon by night. Poetry doth not steal away at dawn of day. But thou must go; good-by for a moment. [*Looks up the orchard path.*] Nay, good-by for all day, for I do spy my guardian uncle.

IDEAL.

Dreams do not end but oft begin at dawn. Give me leave to walk with thee at midday in the Glen of Ferns.

VIOLET.

High noon must be high dream-time when poets love. Await me there to-morrow.

IDEAL.

High noon will brighter grow when thou dost come.

[*Exit* IDEAL.

VIOLET.

As fair spoken a robbery as e'er the sun shone upon. A fair and gallant robber, too, who robs me of my heart in broad daylight, detected in the very act by his own watch. I made the robber tell the hour and minute, so that in any court no cruel alibi could lie. I'm fain to think I'll ne'er again detect so fine a robber. Who's he? What's he? I know not, I care not. I would not ask that question rude and mercenary. I do but know he's the most gentle gentleman I e'er did meet. Oh, if this be love, 't is very kind and sweet!

NORTHLAKE [*afar in the orchard, calls*].

Violet!

VIOLET.

'T is very strange, for I have heard in sundry rhymes, and good rhymes too, that moonlit eves were the only seasons suited for robberies so thinly veiled as this. Why, my own heart doth beat as if there were two hearts within, and I had gained another rather than lost my own. How can it be? But gently, — I 'll not argue the question; 't is much too deep and sweet for idle questioning. Sweet argument, wait for my uncle.

NORTHLAKE [*afar, calls*].

Violet!

VIOLET.

Why, I forgot to ask his name! I could not call him did I wish to, and I might wish, being affrighted. Yet he shall not want so simple a matter; I 'll give him a name. I 'll call him [*commandingly*] Oliver! [*Entreatingly*] Oliver! thy Violet calls thee. [*Indifferently*] Oliver! I do not like the name, 't is too round.

NORTHLAKE [*afar*].

What, ho, Violet!

VIOLET.

I 'll call him Peter. What, ho [*piquantly*], Peter! 'T is too piercing; I 'll none of it. Let me think: I 'll call him [*slowly*] Daniel! Dost hear me [*inquiringly slow*], Daniel? I like it no better than the first. ''I' is too long.

NORTHLAKE [*nearer*].

Where art thou, Violet?

VIOLET.

I 'll call him — yes, I 'll call him Joseph. [*Tenderly*] Joseph! wilt thou not come? Thy Violet calls thee. No, no, 't is a mistake; I 'll not call him Joseph, — 't is too, too flat. I 'll call him — let me see — I 'll call him a name borne by none other, oft dreamed by me, but never met until this morn. I 'll call him my Ideal, my dear, dear Ideal.

NORTHLAKE [*very near*].

Violet! Where can the maiden be? [*Enter* NORTH-LAKE.] I surely saw her going down the orchard path. [*Discovers* VIOLET.] Why, there thou art! Why didst thou not answer me?

VIOLET.

Didst thou call me?

NORTHLAKE.

Did I call thee? Why, if I called once, I called thee twenty times. I 'm almost hoarse with calling. Why art thou out at break of day? One might almost think thou wast in love, to rise so early.

VIOLET [*aside*].

That am I.

NORTHLAKE.

Thy lover comes to-day.

VIOLET [*aside*].

I wonder if he knows!

NORTHLAKE.

He's rich, a thorough business man and solid gentleman.

VIOLET.

I don't like solid gentlemen. Who is he?

NORTHLAKE.

A princely merchant in the West, and owner of banks, mills, stores, houses, and lands. Thou shalt have a list of it all made for thee on satin. Profits of business are five hundred thousand a year. Think of it! thy wedding-dresses of white satin!

VIOLET [*abstractedly*].

Shall I have five hundred thousand dresses of white satin a year?

NORTHLAKE.

No, no; thou hast mixed the profits of the business with the number of dresses.

VIOLET.

Are the profits of the business five hundred thousand white satin dresses a year?

NORTHLAKE.

Stop, now; this shall all be explained after thou art married.

VIOLET.

But I'll have it explained before I'm married.

NORTHLAKE.

Be patient, Violet. He will woo thee properly, and explain all things. I am to meet him at the Dolphin Inn to-day. He'll be in a very good humor at my account of thee.

VIOLET.

I'm well enough without his good humor. Pray, what's his name?

NORTHLAKE.

A merchant prince, the Honorable Hercules Whetstone, Mayor of Cornville.

VIOLET [*laughing*].

What a name! Ha! ha! Couldst thou not add something to it? 'T is too short.

NORTHLAKE.

Thou wilt be added to it.

VIOLET.

That will I not be.

NORTHLAKE.

What's this, — rebellion? Who's been here? Hast thou seen any one in this orchard?

VIOLET.

No one but my Ideal.

NORTHLAKE.

That's too insubstantial.

VIOLET.

More substantial than thou dreamest.

NORTHLAKE.

I'd think thou wast bewitched by love, did I not know thou never hadst a lover.

VIOLET.

That was true yesterday; but to-day! [*Sighing*] Ah, well-a-day!

NORTHLAKE.

Thou speakest truly. Thou hast a lover now, and before the night passes thou shalt see him.

VIOLET.

Shall I?

The Merchant Prince

NORTHLAKE.

He 'll be weary from his travels, and to-day, no doubt, will require rest; but he 'll meet thee to-night at the masked ball. Come, then, to the villa, so that to-night thou mayst appear refreshed.

VIOLET.

I 'm not weary. Oh, that sweet, sweet tree!

NORTHLAKE.

Why, what 's in that tree? 'T is but an orchard tree.

VIOLET.

I 'll wager thee, 't will bear sweet fruit.

NORTHLAKE.

Why, what a fever thou art in!

VIOLET.

I 'm not in a fever. A child that never ventured in the fields may know a blossom when it sees it.

NORTHLAKE.

Come, thy maid, Ninon, has risen, and awaits thee. Thy feet are damp with morning dew from the grass.

VIOLET.

The dew of love is in my heart; and that's not damp.

NORTHLAKE.

This comes of teaching thee, from childhood, philosophy in my melancholy moods. I'll never again teach thee philosophy, though I be as melancholy as Democritus, since thou dost use the philosophy I teach thee against thine uncle and teacher, instead of against the world.

VIOLET.

For the good philosophy thou didst teach me, I'll love thee all my days. But, uncle, is this marriage good? 'T were not good, 't were not philosophical.

NORTHLAKE.

Alas, dear Violet! [*Aside*] If she but knew! [*Aloud*] I cannot give thee thy dues except by this marriage. Thou wast my favorite sister's only child; and when she left thee and thy fortune to my guardianship, I promised to protect thy fortune, and watch over thee even as my own daughter. Now I will get thee a good husband; for he's rich, and a solid gentleman.

VIOLET.

Who's a solid gentleman?

NORTHLAKE.

Why, the Honorable Hercules Whetstone.

VIOLET.

Oh, puzzle thy Whetstone !

NORTHLAKE.

I fear thou 'lt puzzle him, Violet.   But never mind ; come, come now.

VIOLET.

Oh, thou sweet tree ; I cannot leave thee !

NORTHLAKE.

Why, there must be some witchery in that tree ! I 'll have it cut down and burnt.

VIOLET.

Nay, good uncle, thou wouldst not have the tree cut down.   'Tis a good and thrifty tree that never did harm to any one, and therefore I love the tree. [*Takes his arm.*] Dear uncle, do not cut it down.   Thou art a good, dear uncle, and I will go with thee ; and thou wilt let the tree live.

NORTHLAKE [*going*].

Well, then, come, come !   I 'll let the tree live.

[*Exeunt.*

SCENE II. — *A pavilion, with view of the sea. Forenoon.*

Enter WHETSTONE, BLUEGRASS, *and* SCYTHE.

SCYTHE.

Who knows but, in the chemistry of Heaven, we, this noble race of men, are but parasites feeding in space upon a crust of earth encompassing a fiery particle!

BLUEGRASS.

What a glorious thing is one of our ordinary mundane cycles of time! 'Tis only a day; and yet it is a legacy too great for the richest man to put in his will. Let no one be so brazen as to attempt to belittle this magnificent star of ours.

WHETSTONE.

Hold! Professor Scythe, is that the so-called sea?

SCYTHE [*examining it with his glass*].

Yonder liquid and corrugated mass is the rumpled outskirts of the sea. In our scientific formula, it is the correlation of a mighty power.

WHETSTONE [*taking glass and examining*].

I can believe you.

The Merchant Prince

BLUEGRASS.

Hercules Whetstone, patron of the arts and sciences, founder and president of the Cornville Academy as a paying investment, and nourisher of its infant civilization, proprietor of the Cornville Eagle —

WHETSTONE.

One moment, Major Bluegrass: that will do for the home market, but not among strangers. I've given you both a summer vacation, so that you may enjoy yourselves, and work harder when you return. Now, look around, store up knowledge, and — I won't deduct the time from your salaries. That's business. But you must be more particular about my titles. Always speak of me to strangers as the Honorable Mayor Hercules Whetstone, the Merchant Prince of Cornville, near the capital of Illinois, — called Hercules after his grand-uncle Hercules, who drove the Indians down the Mississippi. Do you follow me?

BLUEGRASS, SCYTHE.

We do.

BLUEGRASS.

Oh, why was I so long pent up in the heart of a continent? I can remain on land no longer.

SCYTHE [*taking out his note-book and writing*].

Item, — this is important. Major Bluegrass, long pent up in the heart of the American continent, upon his first sight of the sea wishes to swim. This is of great scientific value, as it shows the recurrence, after long deprivation, of an inherited pre-Adamite instinct; for we read that Adam walked, but never that he swam, therefore are we driven to the waters for evidence. It proves the origin of man from the oyster, or some more ancient inhabitant of the sea.

Bluegrass.

I am no fish, nor ever was. I'd rather spring from a rainbow than a pond.

Scythe.

A pond is your rainbow come to earth.

Bluegrass.

I must swim. Oh, Mayor Whetstone, let us all swim!

Scythe [*writing in his note-book*].

The pre-Adamite instinct in the presence of its primary environment manifests increasing ratio.

Bluegrass.

Professor, take your increasing ratio and slide down to the imponderable roots of the sea. I must get out of this prison of clothes, and into the water.

Whetstone.

Major, try to feel comfortable with your clothes on, for you'd soon be imprisoned without them.

The Merchant Prince

BLUEGRASS.

No dungeon of clothes can hold me! What a lofty repose comes over me as I survey yon glittering expanse of water, like a blue field of undulating velvet! A tear of joy I give to thee, O mighty sea!

SCYTHE [*writing in his note-book*].

Item, — he returns a saline tear to the sea, in memory of his pre-Adamite ancestor. This is the pre-Raphaelism of natural selection.

WHETSTONE.

You are my scientist, my threefold Professor of three chairs, — natural science, hygiene, and agriculture, — in my Cornville Academy. Now, to create a money-making hunger for science at the Academy we must popularize it. Therefore, give me the scientific facts about the sea in a popular sort of way, so that all may understand and enjoy them.

SCYTHE.

Its remote abysses are inhabited by the mammoths of natural history and evolutionary philosophy; and vast herds of sea-cattle graze upon its marine meadows, like buffaloes upon the prairies. In fact, our prairies were once the bottom of the sea, and the buffaloes were supposed to have been left when the waters receded.

BLUEGRASS.

Your marine buffaloes must wear anchors around their necks, instead of cow-bells.

SCYTHE.

Not so. Nature always provides for her creatures; for, as birds soaring above the mountain-tops have great wings of feathers, so, on the other hand, these cattle have immense hoofs, of a substance resembling lead, but much heavier than the lead of commerce.

WHETSTONE.

That adds to their commercial value. Major Bluegrass, you're my private secretary, and editor of my Cornville Eagle: what do you know about the sea?

BLUEGRASS.

I only know what I want to see: I want to see the sport the mermaids see down in their prismatic sea homes, drinking out of beautiful sea-shells, while pearls drop at their iridescent feet. Oh, Hercules Whetstone, you are rich! Get me a diving-bell. I'll interview the mermaids for the benefit of the Eagle, scoop our rival, the Hawkeye Observer, and send up the Eagle's circulation ten thousand.

WHETSTONE.

Blue thunder, Major, be calm! Ever since we arrived here you've been as excited as if you expected to see a drove of fairies and hobgoblins jump out of every bush and dance in the air.

SCYTHE.

He may have caught the infection of the season: for it is now the so-called fairies' season of drolleries and bewitchments. It was a delusion of the ancients, and yet it had some scientific basis,—for science shows that this full summer tide heightens and ripens the natural dispositions of men, so that what is most natural in them often seems most strange.

WHETSTONE.

Professor, examine his hygiene, and see if he needs any medicine.

SCYTHE [*feeling his pulse*].

What's this? Why, this pulse beneath my finger is the alarm-bell of a disordered system! Open wide your eyes. [*Looking into his eye.*] What a distended foresight have we here! The pupil of the eye is dilated like an owl's.

BLUEGRASS.

The owl stands for wisdom.

SCYTHE.

Silence! Hold out your tongue! [*He opens his mouth.*] It has an overcoat with a high color. [*Taking out a thermometer.*] The temperature is seventy-two outside [*taking the temperature under his tongue*], and inside, under the shade of the tongue, it is ninety-nine and nine-tenths. Why, we are approaching spontaneous combustion! [*Feeling his forehead.*] And your forehead is as hot as a volcano. Mayor Whetstone, you may in a few hours lose your private secretary.

WHETSTONE.

I cannot afford to lose him yet; save him, Professor, save him!

SCYTHE.

I will obey. The unimpeachable symptoms indicate hypothetical impoverishment of the blood, complicated by a highly inflamed excitation of the nerve-tissues. We must at once build up an iron constitution.

WHETSTONE.

Build him up, Professor, he's too sensitive; make an ironclad man of him, like myself. Give him ribs of iron.

SCYTHE [*presenting two pills*].

Here are two pills of iron. I'm an Eclectic. This in my right hand is the mammoth shell of the Allopathic school, and this in my left, balanced upon a point of my little finger, and no larger than a solitary grain of mustard-seed, is a fine shot of the Homœopathic school.

BLUEGRASS.

I don't choose either of your schools. I belong to the Hydropathic school.

WHETSTONE.

He who will not swallow a school of medicine to save his life, must be made to do so. Here, Professor, while I hold him, give him a schooling.

[*They try to give* BLUEGRASS *an iron pill.*

37

BLUEGRASS.

Friends, have you no philopena? Give me no pill of iron. May you ne'er sleep with down within your pillow! Oh! put me in a pillory, but put no pill in me. Oh! [*They succeed in giving him a pill.*] I'm pilled; the iron has entered my system; how very hard I'll soon lie down upon my little pillow. And thou, hard Whetstone, thus to sharpen Scythe to mow me down! Cæsar was stabbed by the iron daggers of the conspirators, but I am slugged by an iron bolus from the hands of my friends. This is ironical. Alas! I am a pundit; for as a typical representative of the pun, e'en while the iron was in my heart I have doubly punn'd it.

SCYTHE.

The iron that enters your blood gives life, not death. Thus does modern science show her supremacy over ancient passion.

BLUEGRASS.

You speak well. I'm better now. I acquit you both, and greet you as my friends. [*They all shake hands.*] What a weird place for a marine poem! Would that a seamaid I might be made to see!

WHETSTONE.

Hold on; I have it.

SCYTHE.

What?

WHETSTONE.

Sea-cattle, Professor: they live?

SCYTHE.

Most profoundly! Among wild cattle are the sea-lion, sea-elephant, sea-unicorn —

WHETSTONE.

Stop! We must get a so-called unicorn for the Cornville Aquarium.

SCYTHE.

Among domestic cattle, vast droves of sea-pigs — in our inland nomenclature called porpoises — appear upon its surface when the sea boils, before a storm; and sea-calves, sea-cows, and sea-oxen roam its salt sea pastures.

BLUEGRASS.

This is the romance of science.

WHETSTONE.

We must land them!

SCYTHE.

What do you purpose to do with the porpoises and other sea-cattle?

WHETSTONE.

How little you know of the grand possibilities of business! Why, I'll build up a new industry on these shores. I am the Merchant Prince of Cornville. Here I'll be a sea-cattle king; I'll make a fresh fortune in my gigantic monster emporium for salted sea-cattle. And now to the Dolphin Inn, where I'm to meet Northlake. Then for business by the sea. [*Exeunt.*

The Merchant Prince

Act the Second.

Scene I. — *On the seashore. Afternoon.*

Enter Whetstone, Bluegrass, *and* Scythe.

Whetstone.

Well, boys, I've seen Northlake, and we've all had a good dinner.   A good dinner is also a good romance. Never despise money.   Do you follow me?

Bluegrass, Scythe.

We do.

Whetstone.

Then let us come to business at once.   I've brought you out here to have a consultation, and to get your opinion on certain things, each in his own department of learning, according to the salaries I pay you.   I've arranged to do a fine piece of business.   I'm a man of business, and I'm a man in love.   I'm in love with my business, and I'll make a business of my love.   Professor, how should a man dress to be a so-called lover?

Scythe.

That depends; but this is true: He that loves is like a traveller between the north and south poles, and he will need different suits of clothing, and philosophy.

BLUEGRASS.

What an explanation ! [*laughing*] ha–ha–ha !

WHETSTONE.

Professor, what is the laugh ?

SCYTHE.

My analysis of the laugh is not yet completed, and I am now seeking to produce the missing link. However, the juxtaposition of two incongruous yet contemporaneous images in the mind is simultaneous with contrasting and varying pressures upon the electrically charged nerves. These varying pressures by reflex action cause the pleasurable action of the muscles called the laugh. Let me illustrate. By varying and alternating pressures upon the electrically charged nerves of the eye there is presented to the mind the image of a lover caressing a maiden; and just beyond, the one view overlapping the other, we see a donkey eating the lover's bouquet, and then [*laughing*] ha–ha–ha !

BLUEGRASS.

The donkey took the bouquet for an offering of beau's hay.

WHETSTONE.

Be silent. No trifling with science ! Professor, analyze me Violet.

The Merchant Prince

BLUEGRASS.

I know ! I 'm at home in colors.

WHETSTONE.

Attention !   We 're now in science.

SCYTHE.

The flower violet is the only organic substance in which science has discovered a trace of gold.

WHETSTONE.

Gold and Violet found together, — good !   Why, science is a fortune-teller.   Go on !

SCYTHE.

It is the most refrangible of the seven primary colors of the solar spectrum.

WHETSTONE.

What 's refrangible ?

BLUEGRASS.

I know !

WHETSTONE.

Steady there, Bluegrass !

SCYTHE.

Let me illustrate. You discover by a violet light a beautiful fish in the water, and you wish to catch it. Now, you must throw your hook, dart, or net, not directly at it, but a considerable space this side, according to the depth.

WHETSTONE.

That's fishing under difficulties. Do you mean to say that a man can't see straight in a violet light?

BLUEGRASS.

I know! let me explain.

WHETSTONE.

Listen to the Professor!

SCYTHE.

Violet light passing from one medium into another of a different density becomes most refractory, and turned out of a direct course at an angle : in other words, you must angle for your fish. See my Tables on Molecular Structure, Density, etc., determined by angles of refraction.

WHETSTONE.

So if I get the hang of the angles and depth, I'm all right, am I?

The Merchant Prince

SCYTHE.

In a scientific sense, you are.

WHETSTONE.

Oh, ho! then I'm pretty well posted on Violet. Now for the next point: Professor, what is love?

SCYTHE.

With the passionless precision of science, I say unto you, Mayor Whetstone, though she you love is the most symmetrical duplex pyramidal aggregation of atoms in the human saccharine conglomeration, shun love, and court science; for by spectroscopic analysis of the light proceeding from the eyes of jealous lovers, I have seen their spleen turning a dark green.

WHETSTONE.

I did n't know it was so bad as that! Major, how do you regard love, from the heights of romance?

BLUEGRASS.

A region of enchantment.

WHETSTONE.

Yonder valley with verdure clothed would be a capital place for my emporium for porpoises, or so-called sea-pigs.

BLUEGRASS.

I implore you, Mayor Whetstone, do not project across

44

my mental line of sight that animal, either in its terrestrial or marine form.

WHETSTONE.

He fills his destiny to the full; and besides, he is the most intelligent of animals. It is a historical fact that he was taught to play whist fifty years before the clever dog.

BLUEGRASS.

He jars on the landscape, and is a discord amidst the dulcet harmony of the waves.

WHETSTONE.

What would you have? The good pig eats all he can while he can; therefore he eats like a pig. Major Bluegrass, let me hear no more of your disparaging comments on the honest and assiduous pig,—the most useful and business-like of all our domestic animals. He can nobly hold up his head and represent corn converted. And while he turns the cornfields into bank-notes, shall we blame him if he does not serenade us with the notes of a silver flute?

SCYTHE.

I wish to make a moral observation upon a physical basis: Major, if the formula of your destiny were identical with the pig's, you would give rise to more discordant vocalization than even that disgruntled animal.

The Merchant Prince

He may be the most useful animal upon this magnificent star of ours; but though his good points were as many as his bristles, they could not excuse his shortcomings. The limited geographical prospects of his pen should make him deeply contemplative of the stars; instead of which he roots deeply in the earth. Hence he takes a step backwards, and, instead of increasing his wit, he increases only his weight.

SCYTHE.

Man is like a reversed vegetable that has swallowed its roots and walked off on its branches. Why, what is that at my feet? Let me pick it up tenderly. Hurrah! I've got a geologic pebble! See, Mayor Whetstone, what a rare, grand specimen for the prehistoric museum of the Cornville Academy!

WHETSTONE.

What's it worth?

SCYTHE.

Worth! Mercenary man! Let us reverently take off our hats in its presence. It's worth more than all the property in Cornville. See, Major, see!

BLUEGRASS.

Put it in your pocket, or some one will claim it.

SCYTHE.

Unfeeling man! No one shall claim it. You saw me
pick it up. You are my witnesses.

BLUEGRASS.

To what geologic family does it belong?

SCYTHE.

It is a genuine relic of the cosmic dust. Hurrah! I 've
got a geologic pebble! See the fluted sheets of color per-
vading its interior! It must have been suspended in the pre-
Adamite fires for ages. Gentlemen, remember you have
seen no meteors in the sky.

[*Taking out his note-book and writing.*

Enter SMALL BOY, *crying.*

BOY.

Give me my marble!

SCYTHE.

Why, boy, this is no marble. 'T is a very rare specimen
of the dewdrop form of crystallization, precipitated during the
prevalence of the primeval sand-storms, formed by the cooling
of the stony vapors.

BOY.

Give me my marble, or I 'll call my mother!

47

The Merchant Prince

WHETSTONE.

Professor, you may have picked up the wrong specimen.

SCYTHE.

There can be no mistake. Let me examine it with my microscope. [*Examining it.*] I clearly recognize the uniformity of its circular strata of color, which could be formed only as it revolved on its own incandescent axis in superheated fires. Boy, look through this glass, and then see if you have the youthful cheek to say it is — I tremble to say it — your marble.

BOY [*looking at it through the glass*].

That's my colored marble; I was playing with it. [*To* WHETSTONE *and* BLUEGRASS.] Make him give it back to me, won't you? It has a nick and the first letter of my name on it.

SCYTHE [*surprisedly, re-examining it*].

Why, boy, I cannot afford an unscientific controversy with you or your mother. Alas! take it. [*Giving marble to the* BOY.] And when again you play with it, remember — [*Exit* BOY, *hastily.*] Thus do my hopes of a pre-Adamite museum wither. It was a unique specimen of the circular group of crystallization dreamed of by science, but hitherto undiscovered. Major, here comes your seamaid.

48

Enter CATHARINE *in disguise, with a basket of fish.*

CATHARINE.

Good afternoon, gentlemen landsmen! I have fish in my basket; will you buy? I have your fortunes in my keeping; will you have them?

BLUEGRASS.

I salute you, by the sea, as a near relative in the fields of romance to the milking-maid of our inland pastures.

CATHARINE.

I take you to be landsmen, and, therefore, good fresh men. I am a fortune-teller with varied fortunes. Each summer, for a month, to these shores I come to renew and perfect the spirit's vision, which, even like natural sight, is cleared by good free air and sunshine; and as men with glasses have seen ten hundred living things upon a pin's point, so I, with spiritual lenses, have seen the past, present, and future, each in proper order, marshalled upon a space no larger than a spectacle glass.

WHETSTONE.

Pardon me, — your name and home?

CATHARINE.

My name is Catharine, and my home is wherever I am. I come from the city, where there are more sharks in one day than you will see here in a year, and where people in despair come to me for the fortune fate has denied them. I am more pitiful than fate; and their pleased looks give me a joy greater than does their pittance. Hence, poor souls, I give them precious pictures of future good, which, believing in, they achieve, and thus their griefs assuage.

BLUEGRASS.

We all, to-day, bear our fortunes lightly.

CATHARINE.

And may you at nightfall bear them as lightly! Fine weather makes quick friends. Come, then, gentlemen, will you buy? Each one in his own humor. If there be a true merchant among you, I will tempt him with the fish's weight; if there be a moralist, with the fish's moral; if there be a scientist, with the fish's complicated structure; if there be a poet, with the fish's most poetical history; if there be a gourmand, with the fish's flavor. Each one shall see in the fish he buys, his own humor. He shall have both weight and moral; for a good moral without weight is immoral, and a good weight without a good moral is a dull measure. You shall pay me for the weight, for that the fish had in the sea; but for the moral, that is in my humor, and gain has taken a vacation. Every one has his pastime, and no one is so poor but he has his humor. Mine is to see men buy a fish, each in his own humor; for by the fish's scales will I weigh him.

SCYTHE.

How came your hair so white at your age ?

CATHARINE.

With losing of my husband, and giving of good fortunes. But come, gentlemen; fair weather makes quick friends, but unfair questions, like unfair weather, part them. Will you buy ?

BLUEGRASS.

Let us buy.

WHETSTONE.

Let us first learn the price of the fish.

BLUEGRASS.

It sounds to me like a romance. Come, let us all sit here in pleasant converse; the night is afar, and while we buy we'll enjoy the aroma of the salt-sea zephyrs blown from off the invisible flower-beds of the sea.

WHETSTONE.

Stop your perpetual romance !

BLUEGRASS.

Romance that is not perpetual, but goes by fits and starts, is not worth the reality it feeds upon.

The Merchant Prince

WHETSTONE.

I 'd put the price on everything, — trees, fences, houses, the baby's rattle, and in its first primer a price-list of its expenses.

BLUEGRASS.

Hercules Whetstone, Mayor of Cornville, there are some things upon this magnificent star of ours that are not in the market, — things so high that you cannot reach and put a price upon them in the cold-blooded shambles of merchandise.

WHETSTONE.

There you go again, trying to throw star-dust in your benefactor's eyes. Oh, why did I make you editor of my Cornville Eagle?

BLUEGRASS.

Because your Eagle was asleep, and I was the only one who could wake him up and make him soar into a higher circulation. He looked like a whipped buzzard that had dulled his talons upon old newspapers; but I put new life into him; and now that I have made you the proprietor of a newspaper which is a household word, and which will be in every scholar's library at the close of human learning, you scoff at me. Such is glory in a commercial age! Columbus may discover, but the merchant Americus gives his name to two continents.

SCYTHE.

Good woman, some undesirable chemical change may take

place in your fish. I would advise you to put some salt on them. I am a chemist.

CATHARINE.

The fish are dead; they cannot hear.

SCYTHE.

Mayor Whetstone, why do you not change the Eagle to the Hawkeye Review of Western Science?

BLUEGRASS.

Strip that proud bird of his plumage, and in less than seven revolutions of this magnificent star of ours he will have fewer followers than a vanquished rooster.

WHETSTONE.

Major, I cannot resist you. You are my true, my great and only editor. Give me your hand; let us be friends.

BLUEGRASS.

Now let us go on with our romance. [*To* CATHARINE.] Bring on your fish!

CATHARINE.

There are as queer fish inside as outside the basket, I'll warrant you. [*She presents the basket to* WHETSTONE; *he selects a codfish.*] That is a fish in weight and look of much import,—the codfish. He is an aristocrat among the shoals and schools, and he has done much to build up our own aristocracy. [*She presents the basket to* SCYTHE, *and he selects a Holothurian.*]

SCYTHE.

Why, madam, this is a rare fish, a Holothurian, vulgarly called a sea-cucumber, from its resemblance to that common garden vegetable. I'll mount its skeleton at once. It is the fish of science, and has the power of analysis; for 't is written that when attacked, for self-protection it will divide itself into many pieces, or turn itself inside out.

She presents the basket to BLUEGRASS, *and he selects a flying-fish.*

BLUEGRASS.

How beautiful !

CATHARINE.

Yes, 't is a flying-fish, which, rising above the heavy and obscurer element of its kind, and using its fins as wings, in aërial courses, sparkling like a jewel, beholds the glittering and sunlit scenery of the upper air. There is much similarity between these excursions and the poet's fancies. And as these lower creatures in their airy flights excite the wonderment of fishes and please men, so may human excursions in the higher element of fancy excite the wonderment of men and please the gods.

BLUEGRASS [*in admiration*].

Madam, consider yourself engaged as sea-side correspondent of the Cornville Eagle: topic, sea-fish and their morals. Please accept my card, and draw upon me for a month's salary. [*Gives his card.*

SCYTHE [*writing in his note-book*].

Item,—this is important. In evolution, the grasshopper sprang from the flying-fish.

WHETSTONE.

What birds are those flying above the waves and darting like flying squirrels?

CATHARINE.

They are the larks of the sea, and in the wake of a ship are wider awake than your land larks.

BLUEGRASS.

Madam, with your permission,—upon the first streak of dawn our common meadow-lark has been known to climb the heavenly vaults above this magnificent star of ours like a morning-glory of song.

WHETSTONE.

Professor Scythe, explain.

SCYTHE [*examining the birds with his glass*].

Leaving, for a moment, grave mysteries of the deep upon the floor of the abysmal sea, we ascend to trace in the flight of a simple bird its name and family. The wings of the bird are the pre-Adamite forefeet of an animal which, through ceaseless efforts of evolution, became crowned with feathers. From the movements of these feathered forefeet we can tell all about the bird. Now, Mayor Whetstone, take this glass. [*He gives glass to* WHETSTONE, *who follows the movements of the bird with it.*] Now watch closely the parabola of dip or curve of flight that puts it in the great family of web-footed water-fowls. See the unwavering scoop, the practiced and web-footed ease with which it grazes a wave. We have before us a genuine sea-gull.

WHETSTONE.

Major, put that in the Eagle, and see how it looks in print. Something's bitten me! it must be one of your sea-fleas.
[*Looking up his sleeve.*

BLUEGRASS.

Sea-flea; do you see it?

CATHARINE.

To see a flea, you must flee the sea, — unless perchance you may see a deep-sea flea such as I have at the bottom of my basket. [*Takes out a lobster.*] This is the wicked flea the fisherman pursues. He will give a biting relish to your codfish. [*Offers lobster to* WHETSTONE, *who draws back.*

WHETSTONE.

Is he dead?

of Cornville.

CATHARINE.

Such is his seeming.

WHETSTONE.

What a monster! [*Observing the lobster.*] Professor, what's his scientific history?

SCYTHE [*weariedly*].

I don't know.

WHETSTONE.

Don't know! Professor, it cost me a heap of money to build my nursery of learning, the Cornville Academy, and I'm going to make it the biggest paying institution on this broad continent. I've advertised you in letters big as fence-posts as our own prided prince of science, engaged at an enormous salary. There are already applications for next term from over five hundred anxious fathers of wonderful sons. Can I afford to disappoint them? No. Can you stand there and calmly tell me you cannot give me so simple a thing as the history of a deep-sea flea?

SCYTHE [*looking at lobster with his glass*].

In the race for life, he first made his appearance in the epoch of the mammoth, anterior to the gigantic antediluvians, before the apparition of man upon the earth, and at a season in the progressive series of pre-Adamite evolution soon after the separation of the crocodile branch from the main stem, about forty-five millions of years ago.

57

The Merchant Prince

WHETSTONE.

Astonishing! so long as that?

SCYTHE.

I will not in detail give his scientific biography. It is sufficient that during this period he gorged himself with the blood of these primeval mammoths, which accounts for his size, and often, frenzied by the harrowing appetite of this parasite, these gigantic and prehistoric brutes made the primeval forests for a hundred miles ring with their helpless bellowings. But I will not further excite your pity for the remote ages.

WHETSTONE.

Go on, Professor, go on!

SCYTHE.

This was the summer of his race; but, alas! then came the glacial period. He was frozen up with the mammoths, and remained so for probably twenty millions of years; but such was his tenacity of life, that when the world thawed out, he again appeared, his skin somewhat hardened by exposure, — a fact which you will recognize, — but otherwise cheerful, and in his usual health. Well may his kind be grateful; for, wrapped in ice for æons of time, he was the slender thread upon which their future hung.

WHETSTONE.

But why did he take to the sea?

SCYTHE.

After the apparition of man upon the earth he was driven into the sea by the excited inhabitants.

WHETSTONE.

Major, this is truly wonderful. The Academy will succeed.

BLUEGRASS.

'T is the very romance of science.

WHETSTONE.

But, Professor, what was the glacial period?

SCYTHE.

Well, sir, the glacial period was an epoch when, from a business point of view, ice was cheaper than dirt. Had the apparition then occurred, man could have gone all over the globe on skates. But as it was a vast ball of ice, he would probably have slipped off into space, and nothing more would have been heard of him. And so this star of ice for countless ages rolled on through the sky like a big snow-ball; but at last the great electric sun struck the earth on the equator, which accounts for the equatorial bulge which exists to this day. Then commenced the greatest drama of the elements ever witnessed upon our planet. The vast ice-fields were riven in twain, with terrific reports which reverberated through the heavenly spaces, and to which our present thunder is but as an elemental whisper. Icebergs formed, and in fantastic

59

The Merchant Prince

and sublime shapes, towering mountain high and illuminated by the sun, floated down towards the equator.

WHETSTONE.

Go on, don't stop; go on.

SCYTHE.

Then commenced the great oscillation of the land-masses; then the eruptive rocks and sedimentary strata were moved from their foundations. Then occurred the geologic epoch of the denudation and washdown of hills and mountains, and then were formed the ocean floors, the islands, and the continental areas which we inhabit.

WHETSTONE.

Put that in the Eagle. [*The lobster clings to him.*] Hello! What's the matter now? Professor! Major! Woman! Take off your flea!

BLUEGRASS.

Be a hero!

WHETSTONE.

Great thunder! take him off. He has claws to his eyes. [*Takes off his coat, with the lobster clinging to it.*] Major, this is your fault. Don't speak to me again until you apologize. Come, Professor.

[*Exeunt* SCYTHE *and* WHETSTONE *carrying his coat with lobster clinging to it.*

CATHARINE.

Fair is your prairie wit, and these sea-scenes have keen spices which well try its mettle. He that is young and fresh shall have the salt of experience. Many that come here to be salted by the sea are seasoned by love. Would you be so seasoned?

BLUEGRASS.

If it be a fair, good seasoning.

CATHARINE.

At yonder villa by the sea I well know Mademoiselle Ninon, a French maid who is in friendly service to one Violet. She has a dainty wit, with a foreign flavor that will season you well.

BLUEGRASS.

Acquaint us. I would be so seasoned.

CATHARINE.

To-day she comes that I may tell her fortune. Be at the masquerade to-night; wear a blue ribbon, — there you shall meet her. Trust me. Fare thee well.

[*Exit* CATHARINE.

BLUEGRASS.

This is genuine romance. 'T is sweeter than ambrosia. Oh, why was I so long pent up in the heart of a continent?

Farewell, dull facts of business which have stung me sharper than thistles. Roll on, magnificent star, and bring night and romance. [*Exit.*

Scene II. — *Portico of the Dolphin Inn.*

Enter Whetstone *and* Bluegrass *in conversation.*

Whetstone.

Northlake is a most melancholy man. I believe if he had a warehouse full of anchors, and the market for anchors was booming, he'd be hopelessly unhappy. Said I to him, to-day: Northlake, don't look so confoundedly gloomy; cheer up! the day I marry your niece Violet, you shall have five hundred thousand dollars.

Bluegrass.

His villa looks like the residence of a prince.

Whetstone.

So it does; but it is covered with a mortgage from cellar to roof. One month ago Northlake was a rich man, but, leaving his books and plunging into speculation, he lost not only his fortune, but also that of his niece Violet, who is an orphan, and whose fortune was intrusted to his keeping. Her loss seems to trouble him most.

62

of Cornville.

BLUEGRASS.

When did you become acquainted with him?

WHETSTONE.

Last summer, when they were travelling in the West.
I had some business with him, and I then got a glance at
his niece. I have since corresponded with him. When I
met him to-day he had a book in his hand. I asked him,
What's that book? He replied, It's a work on speculative
philosophy. Said I, Throw it away, and study the market
quotations and crops; that's the kind of speculative philosophy you need.

BLUEGRASS.

What did he say to that?

WHETSTONE.

He opened his book and commenced reading. Said I:
Close your book. I don't understand it, and I don't want
to. I've made you a business proposition that's worth more
than all your books. I've got the booty, and you've got
the beauty. Is it a trade?

Enter PUNCH, *who tries to overhear the conversation.*

BLUEGRASS.

How did that impress him?

63

The Merchant Prince

WHETSTONE.

He replied, You shall have her, but you must first woo her as a tender and gallant lover should, and thus win also her dower of tenderness and fancy.

BLUEGRASS.

How did that strike you?

WHETSTONE.

Oh, said I, I'll show my good points. I'm rich, noble, and good; she'll have me.

BLUEGRASS.

How did that affect him?

WHETSTONE.

Come, Whetstone, said he, you're a practical man. The most practical man in love is the most fanciful. Come to the masquerade to-night in a heroic character. — And I'm going.

BLUEGRASS.

What kind of a hero will you assume to be?

WHETSTONE.

Oh, any kind, just so it's a hero. I can outdo any of them.

BLUEGRASS [*perceiving* PUNCH].

Hello! my friend, can you tell us where to get masquerade suits?

PUNCH.

Yonder, gentlemens. [*Pointing to a neighboring shop.*] i recommends him. He is a good neighbor and an honest man. Good day, gentlemens.

[PUNCH *slips into his shop by a side door.*

WHETSTONE [*reading the sign over the door*].

Peter Punch. Masquerade Suits and Unk-Weed Liniment. For sale or rent. — That's a queer sign!

BLUEGRASS.

They are well suited; for the liniment is a lining under the suits. [*They enter the shop by front door.*

SCENE III. — *A costumer's shop.* PUNCH *arranging his costumes.*

Enter WHETSTONE *and* BLUEGRASS.

PUNCH.

Walk into mine shop, gentlemens. You do me great honors.

WHETSTONE.

Are you not the same man we met outside?

5 65

The Merchant Prince

PUNCH.

Did he say I was honest?

WHETSTONE.

You have it.

PUNCH.

Mine good friends, that was mine brother.

WHETSTONE.

Why, you have the same marks.   What are you up to?

PUNCH.

Mine friend, we were born twins; our own father could n't tell us apart.

BLUEGRASS.

Nature must have been in a proud mood when she duplicated you.

WHETSTONE.

What 's your name?

PUNCH.

Peter Punch.

WHETSTONE.

What 's your brother's name?

PUNCH.

Peter Punch Number Two.   We are twins; I swears it. Mine friends, these are my beautiful suits; and in this bottle is the wonder of seven hemispheres, the sublimely famous and justly celebrated unk-weed liniment. By your firesides, rub it in well. With one wing of medicinal gum, and the other of healing balsam, it flies to its proud home in the bones. Gentlemens, rub it in well. There it works its marvels. This, gentlemens, is the unk-weed art gallery [*pointing to two pictures*]. This one is before taking; that one, after taking. Gentlemens, rub it on your skins inside, and put one of my suits on the outside, and then you do marvels. I swears it.

WHETSTONE.

Which do you sell or rent, — the suits, or the liniment? [PUNCH *winks an eye.*] Why do you wink?

PUNCH.

Goodness gracious! you surprises me so. Mine eyelid slips down. Gentlemens, I cannot rent the wonderful unk-weed.

BLUEGRASS.

Peter Punch, you are a compound fraction. Give your doctor fraction a quick drop, and your tailor fraction a fresh seaming. We have good sound characters, but you and your tailor's goose may mend them. I wish to cast upon a French maid a romantic spell, something in the aurora borealis fashion.

PUNCH.

Gentlemens, I have n't got it [*winking his eye*].

The Merchant Prince

BLUEGRASS.

Why do you wink?

PUNCH.

Mine friend, it is my little weakness. I swears it.

BLUEGRASS.

Try to keep your blind up. It makes me suspicious that something wrong is going on inside. Peter, have you a rainbow suit?

PUNCH.

Mine dear friend, I 've just what will suit you. I made it for a gentlemans just like you, but it rained and he didn't call for it.

BLUEGRASS.

He was only a fair-weather beau; but I 'll be a rainbow as well. [PUNCH *shows him the suit.*] That will suit. Now show me a mask. [PUNCH *shows him a mask.*] Why, it has a nose upon it like a barn-gable.

PUNCH.

Mine friend, a big nose makes a strong character [*laying his finger along his nose*].

BLUEGRASS.

Its cheeks are smooth as a boy's.

68

PUNCH.

Mine friend, how would a rainbow look with a beard on it? Oh, mine friend!

BLUEGRASS.

Come out from under your disguise, Peter Punch. You have the eternal fitness of things under your thumb, and that makes a good tailor and a shrewd philosopher.

PUNCH.

I thank you, gentlemens.

WHETSTONE.

Show me some clothes worn by kings, princes, and potentates.

PUNCH.

Mine friend, let me take your measure. [*He takes* WHETSTONE'S *measure with a tape-line.*]

WHETSTONE.

Do you think you can take my measure for a suitable character suit with your puny tape-line? Put up your line, and search Flatpuddle Smith's Biography of Great Men, — although I must say there are in that book some of the biggest measures of the littlest men on earth; and besides, old Heavyweight, who made his fortune putting sand in sugar, is on the first page. They asked for sugar, and he sandpapered them. It'll go rough with him. Peter Punch, listen to my measure. I 'm a merchant prince, Mayor Whetstone, from Cornville, near the capital of Illinois, called Hercules after my grand-uncle Hercules, who drove the Indians down the Mississippi.

PUNCH [*presenting a robe*].

This is the robe that Julius Cæsar wore when he did thrice refuse the crown up at the Capitol.

WHETSTONE.

Why did he refuse it? Did n't it fit him? I don't want that.

PUNCH [*presenting a suit*].

This is a suit worn by a shepherd boy as he tends his flocks, — young Norval's suit.

WHETSTONE.

Confound you! Do you think I want to be a shepherd boy, and herd sheep?

PUNCH [*presenting another suit*].

This is the suit of a Highlander.

WHETSTONE.

That 's high-sounding. Let me see it. What 's this?

PUNCH.

That goes around the waist like a petticoat.

WHETSTONE.

Where 's the other part ?

PUNCH.

There is none.

WHETSTONE.

Take back your Highlander. [PUNCH *winks.*] Stop winking !

PUNCH.

Goodness gracious! you surprises me so. But here, mine friend. This is a suit of King Richard the Lion-Heart, who slew thousands of Saracens in one day.

WHETSTONE.

Why did n't they stop him, the old villain ? Peter Punch, you may as well put down both shutters over your eyes. Business is closed.   [*Going.*

PUNCH.

Wait, wait, mine dear friend ; I have a beautiful suit of armor, magnificent! I saves it for you. I keeps it wrapped up. It is the suit of a grand knight-errant. [*Takes covering from mounted suit of armor.*]

WHETSTONE.

Ah, that 's something like the thing. The business we are on is a sort of a night errand. What line of business was he in ? Did he travel much at night ?

71

The Merchant Prince

PUNCH.

Mine friend, you is mistaken. The knight-errant was a great man who went around foreign countries clad in a suit of mail, rescuing beautiful damsels, over seven hundred years ago.

WHETSTONE.

So long ago as that? His clothes must be a little rusty; but you can rub them well. You don't say the suit is seven hundred years old?

PUNCH.

Over seven hundred years, mine friend [*winking*].

WHETSTONE.

Major, what would they say if they knew of this in Cornville? So the old rascal used to go around in the night, rescuing beautiful damsels; and they called them night errands! Did n't he rescue the ugly damsels too?

PUNCH.

History is silent, mine friend.

WHETSTONE.

Well, I do declare! I 'll keep up his trade. I 'll build up the old industry on these shores, and I 'll make it hum.

PUNCH.

I have English, French, Spanish, and other cheaper kinds; but I 'll give you the suit of a grand German knight-errant, because he was a great Teuton.

-2

WHETSTONE.

What is the rent to-night for the so-called Teuton knight errant?

PUNCH.

You shall have him cheap. I will calculate. One cent a year, one dollar for each hundred years, — seven dollars, mine friend.

WHETSTONE.

Is n't that tooting it rather high for a night errand?

PUNCH.

Mine friend, the Teuton knight-errant was the most substantial and high-toned.

WHETSTONE.

Substantial and high-toned! I 'll invest. I 'll wake up your old Teuton knight-errant, and make him hum.

[*Exeunt.*

SCENE IV. — *A street. Evening.* JACK, *disguised as an ape, on his way to the masquerade.*

Enter FOPDOODLE *and* TOM, *his valet.*

FOPDOODLE.

By Jove, what is it? — Tom, my man, stand firm. — Audacious creature! So much hair on it, you know. I 'd kindly thank you for your card.

The Merchant Prince

JACK.

Apes and conundrums, having been made before pockets, do not carry their cards. Did you ever husk an ear of corn?

FOPDOODLE.

Audacious beast! Fopdoodle's no farmer.

JACK.

Then how do you expect to husk me by the ear? For the ear of an ape stands higher than a vegetable.

FOPDOODLE.

What a misapplication of terms!

JACK.

Why did you not bring your shell with you?

FOPDOODLE.

What shell?

JACK.

The shell of a goose-egg. Go get it, and put yourself in it, or I'll make an omelet of you by assault and battery.

[*Moving around* FOPDOODLE.

FOPDOODLE.

By Jove, you're a ferocious ape. I'll have you arrested. Ho, there! Oh, policeman, come at once, I pray you, and quell this riot. Come, I command you. But he don't come. What an abominable government we do have! If we had a king, then I'd be protected, — a nice, sweet king! Then, you know, I'd go to court; then I'd be My Lord Fopdoodle. Oh, I'd dearly love a king.

JACK.

What would you do if an enemy arose?

FOPDOODLE.

Why, then the king would say: Upon the breeze that blows upon the borders of my land, I sniff the enemy. My lord, my good and trusty Lord Fopdoodle, hasten. Gather two hundred thousand men or so of our confiding yeomanry and stanchest citizens. Go put the enemy down. — And I would do it.

JACK.

But suppose he would n't stay down?

FOPDOODLE.

Tom, my man, stand firm. — When a king puts an enemy down, he puts him under ground.

JACK.

How would you raise the cash?

FOPDOODLE.

If I saw the treasury running low, I'd rise and thus address the throne of majesty: Of late, most able king, thy servant,

Lord Fopdoodle, whom thou hast ennobled, hath observed sundry of his former friends, shopkeepers, swelling with wealth and aping his nobility. I'll strip them of their towering ambition by taking off the goods from their top shelves. And then the king would say, Good my lord, thou art aright; go thou and do it. And I would go and do it.

JACK.

Would you have any whims?

FOPDOODLE.

Would n't I have whims! — Tom, my man, stand firm. — Thousands of them. If a king and his lords can't have their whims, they 're not so good as other people are. Some day, when the king was in a right good humor, I would say: Your valiant Majesty, an ape doth offend me much. I have a whim. I crave a boon, my liege, a boon, my sovereign; and he would say, I'll grant it thee. Then I would say, I thank thee, good my sovereign. I would that all the apes in thy kingdom were destroyed. And he would say, Take this my signet ring, and let them perish.

JACK.

And you would kill poor Jack?

FOPDOODLE.

Are you Jack? Mr. Northlake's own son Jack, and cousin to beautiful Miss Violet? Why, Jack, I could love even an ape if he were cousin to the beautiful Miss Violet.

JACK.

Would you cozen an ape?

FOPDOODLE.

[*Aside*] I'll steal into Miss Violet's secret heart through this half-open, half-witted gate of a cousin. [*Aloud*] I'm in love. Help me, Jack. About the king, good Jack, I was but joking; and if I were married to Miss Violet, and were the king's lord, I would not hurt a hair on an ape's body. Oh, she's a sweet conundrum; a rose is a conundrum,— why, I'm a sweet conundrum myself. Jack, you're a stunning good fellow, an awfully good ape. Let me stroke ape's hair.

JACK.

Paws off! You Miss my cousin, but she 'll not miss you. I represent to-night a missing link which were well found in you. I'm in full dress,— Nature's regulation costume for the ape; but you commit a barefaced outrage with your ape's nature minus the hair. Meet me at the masquerade.

[*Going.*

FOPDOODLE.

Tom, my man, stand firm!—Don't go, Jack.—I'll go too.

[*Exeunt.*

The Merchant Prince

SCENE V. — VIOLET'S *boudoir, dimly lighted.*

Enter NORTHLAKE, *with domino on his arm, reading a book.*

NORTHLAKE.

Not yet ! still in her dressing-room.   To-night
Fortune shall win a prize more delicate
Than are the velvet leaves of fabled roses.
For years my mind's best nutriment has come
By night, — and what of night ?   I 'll think on it,
While Violet arrays herself for this
Night's masquerade.   It would be right in me
To fancy night as a black sea in space,
That hath circumference and depth, and through
Whose clouded elements grim-visaged hawks
Do sleekly plunge like fishes in the sea,
Seeking their prey ; and all upon the earth
Dwell on the floor of this aërial sea,
And thence look longingly at moon and stars.
Oh, hasten, sun, drive back this monstrous tide
Of night !   See how these trembling night-lights throb
With the sun's offices.   Ten million such
Could not burn up a solitary rood,
Nor make partition for a vaulted league
Of this black night.   But I 'll not rail against
The gentle night ; for often doth it bear
A princely offering to Mammon's shrine.
But come, my niece, my gentle Violet,

Make haste; the hours halt not for lagging maids,
Nor fortune either.

VIOLET [*within*].

Patience, my good uncle.

NORTHLAKE.

What is this vaunted love that so doth set
The world on edge ? 'Tis but the kindled rapture
Of selfishness, that joys to see its double,
Its fond endearment, its sweet concord, and
Reflection in another. While love is true,
Two doubles come, both blent in one, in love's
Bright mirror; but when fails the endearing bond
Of selfishness, the passions, then two natures
Rudely clash therein, and love sees double,
Like to an eye disordered. Wonderful
Nature is solved as easily as a scholar
Doth solve his problem on the wall, when lo !
The master's back is turned, and stealthily
He peeps into the key. O Selfishness,
Thou art the key to all the operations
Of all this globe, — all men and animals,
And all the garniture of fields and forests.
Oft thou art hideous ; then thou art distorted,
As is a lovely body racked by torture ;
But in thy true and fair proportioned self
Thou 'rt beautiful as beauty, and as wise

As wisdom.   Thou art plentiful as color,
Sound, motion; and without thee Nature would
Eclipse herself in stark and blank oblivion.
Learn early this misfortune: Envy and Hate
Live on good fortune. . . .   Not ready yet!
I 'll knock upon the door [*knocking*].   Fair Violet,
Make haste, or we 'll be late.

VIOLET [*within*].

Presently, good uncle.

NORTHLAKE.

Dimly these lights do burn, as if this boudoir
A cloister were; but these fair ornaments,
Arranged in chaste profusion, show a maiden
Mind dwells here that doth delight in beauty.
Yonder, enshrined with wreaths of evergreen
And immortelles, a precious picture hangs, —
Her mother and my sister, looking most
Pityingly on me.   What is this?   Why, here's
The carven image of a maid at prayer;
And here's a tender picture of a youth
And maiden in a flower-garden, done
In placid oils upon a patch of canvas.
Methinks the artist had done better had
He put here in the corner of the picture
Some quaint and curious demon, peeping o'er
The garden wall.   Why, looking at these toys,
So fitting for a maiden's bower, almost

Moves me from my purpose.   Must all these
Vanish?   Will not some angel answer me?
No; Heaven answers not a bankrupt's prayer.
My fortune and her fortune swallowed in
The hideous maw of speculation; both
Banished, completely banished!   Why, I'd rather
Be exiled from my country than my fortune.
But all, all is not lost.   She hath a girlish
Beauty and a heart most rare; and in
This age of rude massed gold there's value in it.
A heaven-dowered woman hath an alchemy
That can refine base gold.   The bargain's good. . . .
Ninon, is not thy lady nearly ready?

NINON [*within*].

My lady does demur to wear ze dress,
And says she'd rather be plain Violet.

NORTHLAKE.

Thy scruples, Violet, are pretty whims;
But more become a simpering maid than thy
Chaste self.   [*Aside*] Alas, the plague of poverty!
[*Aloud*] Thou dost obedient service to thy guardian
Uncle, and mayst save him from a plague
That's worse than all the plagues that e'er beset
The town of Coventry.

VIOLET [*within*].

Plague take the costume!   I do not like it.

The Merchant Prince

NORTHLAKE.

Let me turn up these lights — the jewel's from
                           [Turning up the lights.
Its casket brought. I keep no false coin in
My house, no cunning mockery, no smirking
Counterfeit. Why, he shall own, and rightly
Own, that she, in bodily volition,
Movement, and gesture, well doth match a mind
That's matchless.

Enter VIOLET *in fancy costume, and* NINON *carrying domino.*

VIOLET.

Dear uncle, art thou pleased?

NORTHLAKE.

Why, thou art richly worth his gold, were his
Possessions fabulous.

VIOLET.

      Whose gold, good uncle?
Thou speakest strangely.

NORTHLAKE.

      I did but jest a trifle.

VIOLET.

Give me thy arm, good uncle. I'll tease thee.
                           [Taking his arm.
I do mistrust thou'dst sell me in this costume;

For Ninon, chatting as we dressed, and humoring
Me, did say that often thus they sell
Circassian maids unto the Turk.

NORTHLAKE.

Nay, 't is but idle prattle in Ninon.

VIOLET.

Dear uncle, let Ninon companion be
To me to-night.

NORTHLAKE.

If 't is thy merry wish.

VIOLET.

I thank thee, my dear uncle.

NORTHLAKE [*taking domino from* NINON *and putting it
on* VIOLET].

Give me the domino.   Thou 'lt wear it on
Thy passage to the ball.   It is a shield
Which, laid aside, thy beauty's peerless might
Shall conquer all.

[*Curtain.*

The Merchant Prince

Act the Third.

Enter WHETSTONE *and* BLUEGRASS *in masquerade costume.*

WHETSTONE.

Major, have we any parallels for this?

BLUEGRASS.

Millions of parallels. Nature loves a masquerade as much as she abhors a vacuum.

WHETSTONE.

See if my character is loose. It feels like slipping down over my boots.

BLUEGRASS.

Hold on to your character; never let it slip, or all is lost. Remember, you are a Teuton knight-errant of the Horn of Plenty, and I am Rainbow, your squire. The ancient warrior Achilles carried a shield with amazing scenes beaten thereon.

WHETSTONE.

I can beat Achilles' shield all hollow. I've brought my album, with photographs of my houses, stores, banks, farms, academy, and prize cattle. Here it is. [*Displaying a large album.*] But come, my boy, again explain. Why am I called the Horn of Plenty?

BLUEGRASS.

Horn of Plenty signifies wealth. Remember, we are now walking in a romance, and explanations are like stumbling-blocks in a dream. One must imagine more than he sees.

Enter SCYTHE *with glass, examining* WHETSTONE, *and especially* JACK, *among the masqueraders.*

WHETSTONE.

Then she might imagine I was a dinner-horn, a trombone-horn, a tooting-horn, the moon's horn, a horned beast, or some other horn, or that I took a horn as a matter of business.

BLUEGRASS.

Don't talk of business; stick to your character.

WHETSTONE.

Confound you, my boy! I am sticking to my character, and my character sticks to me. I feel like a rooster in an iron nightgown.

BLUEGRASS.

Solid in solid.

WHETSTONE.

I'm the only one here who seems to have his clothes riveted and anchored to him.

85

BLUEGRASS.

Hold! you must talk in the language of knight-errantry :
My sweet, fair, or beauteous lady, wilt tread a measure in
the dance ? I am listed in the tournament of love. — Something in that strain.

WHETSTONE.

Will my clothes bear the strain ?

BLUEGRASS.

Seemingly, but if you should feel rusty, either in character
or memory, ask me to polish you ; for such is my traditional
duty as your faithful squire.

Enter NORTHLAKE, VIOLET, *and* NINON.

WHETSTONE [*observing* VIOLET].

Oh, ho! look there, Major, my boy, — there comes the
prize of the market. She 's pretty as a pet kitten. She 's
sweet as a box of honey. She 's worth a barrel of money.
I wish it were Violet; I 'd throw in the farm on Pearl
Creek.

BLUEGRASS.

Steady, steady ; hang on to your character!

CATHARINE [*recognizing* BLUEGRASS].

[*Aside*] That is he with the blue ribbon. I 'll hail this
rainbow. [*Aloud*] Sir Rainbow, you make fair promises, and
keep them fairly.

BLUEGRASS.

Rainbows bespeak fair weather and fair maids.

CATHARINE.

You have bespoken fair weather with bright words, and you shall bespeak a fair maid with bright eyes, as I promised you to-day on the seashore.

BLUEGRASS.

Oh, where is she?

CATHARINE.

Yonder she stands while the fates work her destiny, — the fair Ninon.   Come, give me your arm.

[*They join* NINON.

WHETSTONE.

Going, going, gone; knocked down to the first bidder! What a weakness he has developed for women!

NORTHLAKE.

[*Aside*] Why, that's the voice of Mayor Whetstone.   I'll address him.   [*Aloud*] Ho, most gallant knight, thy squire hath left thee in a lonesome plight!

WHETSTONE.

I am the so-called Teuton knight of the Horn of Plenty. Do you know me?

The Merchant Prince

NORTHLAKE.

Have you the mettle of the true knight?

WHETSTONE.

I'm covered with metal seven hundred years old. Northlake, I know you! Where is she?

NORTHLAKE.

Yonder, with her maid. Go, woo and win the lady. You
could not have chosen a better suit in which to press your
suit.

WHETSTONE.

She shall be mine, and you shall be rewarded. [*To* VIOLET.]
Beauteous lady, I am the resplendent knight of the Horn of
Plenty. [*Aside*] What's the rest? [*Aloud*] Please wait a
moment till I see my squire.

> [*He goes to consult with* BLUEGRASS.

NORTHLAKE.

He is the antipodes of that ancient gentleman whose dress
he wears. But, alas! the rudest oft give most thanks for a
gentle wife, and he'll make her a comfortable husband. To
do this, some would say was villanous in me; but 'tis a
convenient fashion. Wealth is a rude mountain, from which
the gentle win gentle treasures. The Decorator of the fields
hath placed the flower and sturdy plant side by side, and the
one doth shield the other. From dankest earth the whitest

88

lily grows; from keen-edged sands the fairest blossom blows. E'en frozen clods have flowers, and flowers their frozen clods.

WHETSTONE [*returning to* VIOLET].

Wilt tread a measure with me? I am listed in the tournament of love.

VIOLET.

Thy words bespeak a gallant knight. I'll grant thy wish.

NORTHLAKE [*to* CATHARINE].

I pray thee for a partner.

A dance. WHETSTONE *and* VIOLET, BLUEGRASS *and* NINON, NORTHLAKE *and* CATHARINE; SCYTHE *inspects* JACK *with his glass and takes him for a partner.*

[*Curtain.*

SCENE II. — *A balcony.*

Enter WHETSTONE *and* VIOLET.

VIOLET.

Sir Knight of the Horn of Plenty, did thy grand-uncle slay the Indians?

WHETSTONE.

All of them. The banks of the Mississippi were covered. He had hired soldiers under him who harvested their scalps

The Merchant Prince

while he slew them.   In my life in Flatpuddle Smith's Biography of Great Men, you will find him given as my great collateral ancestor.

Thy family is warlike, but surely thou art a gentle knight.

Oh, I 'm gentle now; but if one of those savage Indians rose up against me, I 'd heap this illustrated album of civilization, like a burning coal, upon his head!   Do you know, when I was in Europe they offered to make me a reigning prince — if I 'd pay for it.   There were several vacant thrones, and I was about making a bid, when my gigantic business interests called me back to Cornville, and the throne fell through.

When you were in Europe, did you visit Rome?

Passed through in the night-time, and did n't stop.   No business done there; only a lot of fellows cutting figures in stone, and painting pictures under the old masters.

'T is cruel in thee to jest so.   Thy figure shows a gallant knight, and thou dost speak by contraries to make thy showing finer.   How doth the moon shine in Europe?

WHETSTONE.

The same old moon.

VIOLET.

'T is very fair.

WHETSTONE.

Why, there is the so-called fair moon now, sure enough!
[*Looking at the moon.*]   It shines like a new tin pan.

VIOLET.

The moon shines on thy armor, and thou thyself dost
shine like a new tin pan.

WHETSTONE.

There's the new moon, the quarter moon, the full moon,
and the dark of the moon.   The moon is good enough in its
place.

VIOLET.

Why, where is the moon's place, if not in heaven?

WHETSTONE.

In the almanac.

VIOLET.

Why, gallant knights and lovers gather substantial suste-
nance from moonlight.   'T is prescribed by Heaven and
the poets.   And thou revilest the moon? Thou art a traitor
to nature.   Thy best place were in an almanac, in the dark
of the moon, in the sign of Capricorn.

The Merchant Prince

WHETSTONE.

Off with the mask! [*Removes head-piece.*] Behold the real Honorable Mayor Whetstone, Merchant Prince of Cornville, near the capital of Illinois; called Hercules after his real grand-uncle Hercules, who drove the real Indians reeling down the real Mississippi. Do you follow me?

VIOLET.

Heaven guide me in this whirlwind of contraries!

WHETSTONE.

Take yours off, too.

VIOLET.

As I hate disguises, and this moonlight is a gentle vapor, I'll unmask without more argument.   [*She unmasks.*

WHETSTONE.

Beauteous Violet, you are my future wife. Let, oh, let me take a kiss.

VIOLET.

Our acquaintance is too brief for a jest so durable.

WHETSTONE.

Come, no one sees us. Just one little kiss. [*Enter* SCYTHE, *looking at them through his glass.*] Professor, get out! Take notes, hunt specimens, and shelve your knowledge; but never let me see you here again. [*To* VIOLET] Did not your uncle tell you?   [*Exit* SCYTHE.

92

VIOLET.

Why, thou art a sportive knight, indeed. Oh, thou art a deep dissembler! But, no, thou art a gallant knight! This is some stratagem of words and dress, invented by my good uncle for my diversion. If thou wilt keep a secret, I will tell it thee.

WHETSTONE.

I'll keep it. But, oh, how I'd like a kiss!

VIOLET.

Kissing is an idle fashion but lightly spoken of by our best authors, and well missed by young misses. But to my secret. This morn my uncle told me in the orchard that he had chosen for me a lover,—a most substantial gentleman, a very merchant prince — [*Pauses.*

WHETSTONE.

Go on; give me all your secret.

VIOLET.

Why, thou art he in name and title; but I know thou art not, from thy discord in guise, speech, and action; and thou dost carry out a jest too literally with thy contraries.

WHETSTONE.

I swear I am the real he. See, here is my album! [*Opening album.*] Here is my picture, in my shirt-sleeves, before my store. See the sign above the door: Hercules Whetstone's Gigantic Store. Here's my banking-house. See, see! Now, do you believe and love me? Be my wife, and I'll bind the bargain with a kiss.

VIOLET.

Surely thou art the prince of jesters; and if 't is thy humor, in part I'll not deny thee; but no maid should bind a bargain with betrothal kiss until she knows the true worth of it. Hast thou any castles in thy domain?

WHETSTONE.

Castles? Why, I own the half of Cornville. See [*showing the album*], here's my town-house. I'll have its hall set in solid mahogany. Then we'll be the Honorable Mr. and Mrs. Mayor Whetstone, of Mahogany Hall, Cornville, solid people, — if you like, in our castle.

VIOLET.

When thou dost in a day change thy house into a castle, then it will have a gallant knight.

Enter FOPDOODLE *concealing himself.*

WHETSTONE [*showing a picture in the album*].

See, this is my stately dairy farm. Yonder pearly stream that through the middle of the farm doth run and wind about, and then run in and out as if 't were playing tag between its wave-kissed banks, is called Pearl Creek. It is a curious stream. Here, once, the wild goose, while he plucked the toothsome grass from its banks of verdure, listened to an Indian maid. Here, beneath this spacious sycamore, we'll sit and fish for speckled trout; I'll bait the hook. And when 'tis winter we'll skate upon it. See yonder latticed arbor perched upon the bank: it is the hen-house, with hens and their companions from many lands. Here will we gather eggs through all the seasons; and to have fresh eggs in winter is no mean luxury. See yonder moss-covered house of stone picturesquely wading in the water. It is the milk-house, with all its crocks of golden cream. Here, with sparkling water, without a murmur from the world, we'll fill our crocks of fortune to the brim. Here, amid these scenes of thrift and beauty, bustling hens, pensive geese, lowing herds, crocks of cream, and gleaming fishes, we'll wander hand in hand, spending our full-orbed honeymoon, while the rude outsiders stare in dreamy wonder at so much happiness on earth. Does not the prospect charm you?

VIOLET.

Do not end thy bright illumined catalogue. Give me it all.

WHETSTONE.

Give you it all! I'll give you your share, but not all. Come, Violet, that's asking too much!

FOPDOODLE [*from his concealment*].

Oh for a dagger to assassinate him! O dazzling Violet!

The Merchant Prince

VIOLET.

Continue.

WHETSTONE.

Oh! Now we leave the country, and come to town [*referring to the album*]. Here is my edifice of learning, my Cornville Academy, my spring of knowledge. I own the whole of it. Here's my Cornville Eagle, which shall brighten its plumage when we are married; and here's my Bank, whose president craves your hand. Do let me take it now; no one is looking.

SCYTHE *appears stealthily for a moment, observing them with his glass.*

VIOLET.

They who love moonlight must not forget the man in the moon; and I must first ask my uncle. But I did not know that knights of late had grown so rich. I must put on my spectacles.

WHETSTONE.

Bless me, are you near-sighted? I'll come nearer.

VIOLET.

Nay, at dawn I was near-sighted, but to-night I am far-sighted.

WHETSTONE.

Bless me, I almost forgot it, — I own half a church, and built the steeple out of my own pocket.

VIOLET.

Art thou a pious knight?

WHETSTONE.

Heaven must have a share. Besides, it was a sharp business project. It is the highest steeple in the State; and some day I'll ride into the governor's chair on it.

VIOLET.

Thy steeple should turn thy thoughts to heaven, instead of to the earth.

WHETSTONE.

That reminds me of the lightning-rod. [*Aside*] I'll give her a sample of my business talents. [*Aloud*] A pedler one day said to me: Mayor Whetstone, I wish to introduce into your community my patent flanged galvanized lightning-rods. Said I to him, pointing to the steeple: Eureka! Excelsior! Do you climb? Do you follow me? Do you donate? Is the advertisement worth the rod? Will you spare the steeple, and spoil the rod? He climbed. He donated. Before the next thunderstorm he received orders for over forty rods from members who were afraid the lightning would strike their property if they did n't buy a rod.

VIOLET.

I much mistrust thou 'rt not a redoubtable, but only a doubtful, knight.

7 97

WHETSTONE [*kneeling*].

Heaven knows 't is true.   I pray for your hand.

VIOLET.

Pray for thine own heart.   Rise ; for when thou kneelest, thou half liest.   So stand up, and be not prone to lie upon thy knees.

FOPDOODLE [*from his concealment*].

Oh, how I want to be a noble husband !   O dazzling Violet !   Oh, oh !

WHETSTONE [*rising*].

I thought I heard some one owe me something !

VIOLET.

No one here owes thee anything.   Take thy mind off thy gains.

WHETSTONE.

Let me call your uncle.

VIOLET.

Nay, thy jest in greed lacks no ingredient.

WHETSTONE.

That 's not all ; I have more stores, houses, cattle, stocks, barrels of money, stacks of it —

VIOLET.

Well, go on ; give me it all.

98

WHETSTONE.

Give you it all!

VIOLET.

All, everything.

WHETSTONE.

Give you it all! That's practical. Who'd have thought it in one so young? Would you outwit me? Would you outmatch me? Would you ruin me?

VIOLET.

Thou art a gentle stupid. I only meant, give me a description of all, — thy catalogue of all thou hast. Thy lips label better thy goods than thy love.

WHETSTONE.

What's that?

VIOLET.

I insist upon all. I do mistrust — for I'm no trusting miss — that thou art a poor ignoble man withal, hired by my jesting uncle withal to put on this chivalrous disguise withal to jest with me withal. What false knight art thou that thou wilt not endow the lady of thy love with all thou dost possess, that lovest thy goods better than love? Thou art of crude metal. Go to thy farm on Pearl Creek; I do not want thy goods.

WHETSTONE.

Am I dreaming?

The Merchant Prince

FOPDOODLE [*from his concealment*].

Oh for a carmine dagger to hack, to stab, to prostrate him! Oh, how I crave to be a noble husband. O dazzling Violet!

VIOLET.

Thou hast kept from thy catalogue and basely concealed that which loving knights and ladies prize the highest.

WHETSTONE.

What can it be? I'll buy it.

VIOLET.

'T were better guessed, for by purchase it loses its value.

WHETSTONE.

I know nothing like it. But if it be concealed and of the highest value, it must be a gold mine.

VIOLET.

Nay, thou gentle stupid, try again.

WHETSTONE.

Ah, now I've got it. A coal mine. Why, Violet, you are wiser than I thought. You look beneath the surface. There is a rich vein of coal beneath my farm; but it's not worked.

VIOLET.

Neither is the vein of love well worked by thee. Try again, and for lack of discovery and my sentence, thou shalt bear no complaint to my uncle.

FOPDOODLE [*from his concealment*].

Oh, let me tell! O dazzling Violet!

WHETSTONE.

I can think of nothing else besides.

VIOLET.

Put thy hand to thy left side. Hast thou no heart?

WHETSTONE [*putting his hand over his heart*].

I have a heart; and oh, I feel it beat tremendously.

VIOLET.

He is a poor merchant in love, who, having a heart, hath no value to it. He's a bankrupt who can declare no dividend unto his lady creditor. A true and loving heart hath larger dividends than banks, richer harvests than farms, finer goods than stores, and more happiness than all the world besides.

FOPDOODLE [*from his concealment*].

O Violet, I've got a heart. O dazzling Violet!

VIOLET.

Methinks that soon the silver moon will yonder mantling cloud enrich, and leave thee a knight quite poor.

WHETSTONE.

I cannot lose you. Your worth grows upon me at the rate of a thousand dollars a minute. [*Kneeling*] Here on my knees let me explain.

VIOLET.

Rise. I cannot help thee, although 't is sadly said. Hadst thou discovered thy heart earlier, and put the true worth of a heart upon it, then I had thought more deeply. But now, alas! thy discovery comes too late. I am a young judge, yet my sentence shall be a just one, and I 'll not revoke it. Thou art a guileful knight. I sentence thee to perpetual banishment; and that thou mayst study the phases of a maid's heart and of the moon, I will allow thee no book but thy almanac.

WHETSTONE.

Let the heavens hear me! I am not through yet. I have a fearful fever!

VIOLET.

Maids are no doctors, except for hearts in love.

WHETSTONE.

Oh, I am in love, and now I know it.

VIOLET.

Thy complaint comes too late. Be patient, but be no patient of mine. I'll practice on thee no further. Thou hast thy sentence.

FOPDOODLE *leaves his concealment.*

FOPDOODLE.

Stay, you villain! If I had my dagger, I'd stab you. O dazzling Violet!

WHETSTONE [*rising*].

Who are you?

FOPDOODLE.

You caitiff knight, I am Augustus Fopdoodle and your deadly rival. O dazzling Violet!

WHETSTONE.

You rascal rat! you eavesdropper! If I had my knightly sword, I'd hack you into a thousand pieces and make you bait for catfish. Where's my sword?

FOPDOODLE.

Aha, vain boaster! There is my gage of battle; pick it up. [*Throws down a glove.*

WHETSTONE.

Pick it up yourself, you villain!

The Merchant Prince

VIOLET.

Hold, gentlemen, brave gentlemen! 'Twere a pity that
two such gentlemen should end a harmless jest in sanguinary
strife. Come. Your brave humors make the rash current of
your words more harmful than your sword-blades. Believe
me. Come.   [*Exeunt* WHETSTONE *and* VIOLET.

FOPDOODLE.

I 'll challenge him this very night to fight a duel. Fopdoodle, thou art a brave man. Bless thee, Augustus Fopdoodle. Bless thee, O dazzling Violet! I am a terribly
quick man, and I should have killed thousands of men had I
but done it when I thought to do it. Let me think.—No,
I must not think so much upon the bloody deed, the grim
and horrid spectacle. Thinking cools me off like an evap-
oration; yet truly there is a manifold vigor in me, O dazzling Violet, else why am I so brave when heated? Fire
brings out my bravery. What is the coward quality that
on a sudden chokes my valor so? I have it: it comes of
too much thinking. Let me pluck it out.—But no, I cannot pluck out my brains; yet I will admonish my head not
to think so much. But still, thinking is wisdom; therefore
too much wisdom makes me a thinking coward. I must
cultivate less wisdom. O dazzling Violet! I 'll send him
a challenge, and he 'll not fight. A bloodless triumph.
Now thinking comes to my rescue. Animals have not this
process of thinking, for I have seen terrible animals fight
ferociously until they were dead, dead. O dazzling Violet!

Therefore I bless thee, Augustus Fopdoodle, that thou hast the spirit of bravery; but I do bless thee more that thou hast the process of thinking. I do not think he 'll fight. O dazzling Violet!

[*Exit.*

Scene III. — *The same.*

Enter Scythe, *with glass. He seats himself in a corner, observes the moon, and takes notes. Enter* Bluegrass *and* Ninon, *who do not observe him.*

Bluegrass.

We have tripped into the hour of midnight, the fairies' hour. Now the fairest face, night-blooming like a mystic flower, may unmask its sweetness.

Ninon.

Charmant! Monsieur Rainbow, you delight me all ze night.

Bluegrass.

Here I 'll unmask, for your two eyes have kindled a flame in my breast such as could not be lighted by all the stars burning in yonder heavens.   [*He unmasks.*

Ninon.

Monsieur Rainbow, you is ze fiery lover, — ze grand gentleman. Take away ze bad mask.

The Merchant Prince

BLUEGRASS.

In the nineteenth century, bright little sister of Venus, I'll unmask you. [*He unmasks and kisses her.*

NINON.

Très joli! Oh, Monsieur Rainbow, you is ze grand American lover.

BLUEGRASS.

You are the sweetest little maid upon this magnificent star of ours.

NINON.

Charmant! Monsieur, you are ze Rainbow more sparkling zan ze wine-cup.

BLUEGRASS.

There is a wine finer than that of the grape to-night. Let this sparkling envelope of air be our distraction. See, Ninon, how it holds this globe like a cup star-jewelled, and proffered to our senses with all its myriad distilments of rapturous motions, varied colors, gladsome odors, and sweet sounds.

NINON.

Monsieur Rainbow, we will drink from zat cup, and hunt ze buffalo in ze West. Magnifique!

BLUEGRASS.

[*Aside*] Beautiful simplicity! Arcadia had no better than this untutored Parisian. [*Aloud*] Dear Ninon, the advance-guard and keen-eyed pickets of civilization have driven the buffalo from our future home in Cornville; but you shall have amusement.

NINON.

[*Aside*] Oh, he is ze grand American lover!

BLUEGRASS.

Ninon, in Paris were you ever courted, — that is to say, were you ever in a court of love or law?

NINON.

Why, Major Bluegrass, I did not know ze court was for ze love. I thought ze court was only for ze law.

BLUEGRASS.

Give me simplicity! O Love, the entangler, do not unravel us! Let no frog croak in Cornville.

SCYTHE *takes a glance at them through his glass.*

NINON.

Très beau! Good Monsieur Rainbow, ze frog is ze great beau in ze springtime, with his fine green coat and gold buttons.

BLUEGRASS.

Now I remember me, the frog has a gallant look when the spring is in the meadows and the banks are grassy. Now I remember me more closely, he also has a romantic look; for once, when a boy, I watched him sitting, like a sybarite Turk, upon a dewy bank in the pale moonlight, enjoying the downward fragrance of an o'erbending lily, which o'er him hung like a wedding bell. He gazed upon the moon sailing above him, and then upon the moon below him, glistening in the pond which was his bed, — Neptune's trundle-bed, made for frogs, — until, between these two perplexities of light, his eyes like diamonds shone. Shall I halt here?

SCYTHE *looks at the earth and moon alternately with his glass.*

NINON.

No, no, dear Monsieur; go on, good Monsieur Rainbow. I have ze grand interest. His eyes shone like ze diamonds, ze beautiful diamonds. Superbe!

BLUEGRASS.

Well, his eyes, like twin solitaires encrusted in rims of red gold, shone more translucently than any that e'er sparkled in the betrothal ring of an expectant bride. It seems this gentleman in green had grown fixedly practical between the real moon and the ideal moon, and would not have an ideal when he had not the real; for he, poor frog, like some of our practical humans, did not know that the ideal moon in a pond was much finer than a pond in the real moon. Now do I see him, as plainly as if it were to-night, there coolly sitting and meditating, quite philosophical.

NINON.

Oui, oui ; zat was a foolish froggie, Monsieur Rainbow. Beware of ze philosophy. Ah, Major Bluegrass, you have ze fervent language zat thrills me.

BLUEGRASS.

Dear Ninon, my description, like your own pretty costume with all its frills, tucks, and love-knots, has a moral with it. Before this philosophic gentleman in green had reconciled himself to an ideal, a flying cloud curtained the moon; and thus in his philosophy he let bright opportunity slip, and went dark below.

SCYTHE *discontinues using glass.*

NINON.

Oui, oui ; too true. I pity ze poor froggie.

BLUEGRASS.

Dear Ninon, render him no pity ; for although I was but a green boy, I then resolved that opportunity was greater than philosophy. Ninon, yonder glorious moon shines brightly as on that memorable night in the meadows. 'T is a bright opportunity ; let me kiss thee again.

NINON.

Pardon, sweet Monsieur Rainbow ; wait for ze grand opportunity when ze honeymoon upon our wedding shines ; then you shall have ze thousand kisses. Charmant ! [*Exeunt.*

SCENE IV. — *The same.*

Enter NORTHLAKE *and* CATHARINE.

NORTHLAKE.

Fair lady, I have led thee to this spot,
Removed from all the merry throng of maskers ;
For love grows best in solitude, and thrives
But poorly when too many eyes look on ;
So saying, I unmask [*unmasking*], and ask that thou
Wilt move that vestment from thy cheek, to whose
Illumined page thine eyes are bright indexes.
Pray let me draw the envious curtain back ;
For though I 've scored some years, yet ne'er 't was said
That I ungallant proved.

CATHARINE.

Stay for a moment, — I am strangely faint.

NORTHLAKE.

The ball-room's heat I fear has wearied thee.
                              [*Tenderly supporting her.*

CATHARINE [*recovering*].

Nay, heed it not ; I long have been aweary.

NORTHLAKE.

Fair lady, tenderest fruit and hidden clings
Within its husk until full season.   Now

Thou mayst remove thy mask, for in my heart
There 's sympathy that makes occasion ripe.

CATHARINE.

I see thou art a gallant gentleman ;
I'd converse hold with thee, but pray that thou
Wouldst leave me to my mask.

NORTHLAKE.

Be it as thou dost wish ;
But at the close of our sweet interview
I beg thou wilt disclose to me the face
Of her whose gentle hand I now do press
With all the ardor of my youthful days.

CATHARINE.

Oh, thou shalt have thy asking, never fear ;
But first thou 'lt answer questioning, — 't is but
A foolish, idle question, yet thou mayst
True answer make.   But to be brief : Didst ever
Love before ?   Good gentleman, I pray thee
Answer me truly.

NORTHLAKE.

Briefly, but once.

CATHARINE.

Speak not beyond.   I thank thee.   Sweeter sound
Was never borne upon the air to woman.
But of this once ?   Answer me that.

The Merchant Prince

NORTHLAKE.

Truly but once, and once most truly, I
Did love her. [*Pausing.*] Well, I 'll pause no further; yet
Her voice and gesture much resembled thine.
We parted, years ago, in sad estrangement;
And though within that sombre lapse of time
We 've often met, yet never have we spoken.
For we indeed are to each other — dead!

CATHARINE.

Dead to each other! 't is a woful word
To those who 've loved. Thou fickle man! thou dost
Deceive thyself, — for true love never dies.
Thy fate doth mirror mine.

NORTHLAKE [*taking her hand*].
      I beg thee tell it me.

CATHARINE.

Thou hold'st my hand close as my husband did
Upon our wedding morn, when he did make
Such noble vows of constancy as troops
Of angels swift delight to register.
And so we lived for many happy years;
They now do seem a vanished paradise;
And, looking back, beyond my later years,
It seems to me as fair as tender Eden
Did unto our first mother, Eve. And oft
I 've wept most burning tears in memory
Of the adored one who did hold me there.

NORTHLAKE.

Why, thou dost clasp my hand with feverish zeal;
Let 's walk upon the cliff.

CATHARINE.

       Nay, stay, and listen.

NORTHLAKE.

I 'll do as thou desirest.

CATHARINE.

Thou art a gallant gentleman. I 'll swift
Unveil to thee a heart that 's worthier
Than is the poor masked face thou pray'st to see.
Oh, how can I portray to thee my joy
When I was wife and mother! Think of it, —
For I am sure thou art a good, true man,
And gallant gentleman. — In my full flush
Of joy I was estranged from my dear husband,
Whom I did love so well I would have pledged
My soul upon his honor. Then I was wild
With sudden doubt and frenzied jealousy.
His goodness seemed but evil, — as by the quick
Hot-bolted lightning blasted, or as poison
Transforms the fairest ornaments. In this
Mad frenzy, at this same hour of midnight,
I fled from him. Since then I 've been a restless
Wanderer on the earth. But, oh! on me
The blame harder doth rest than it doth rest —
On thee!

The Merchant Prince

NORTHLAKE.

On me?   Why, who art thou?

CATHARINE [*unmasking*].

Thy lady Catharine.—Thou gallant gentleman,
I may again return to thee.   Good-night!

[Exit CATHARINE.

NORTHLAKE.

Lost wife, return!   'T is pitiful!   By thee
These lonely years my life's been haunted.   Once
In each year thy visits, like untimely
Seasons, come upon me, when and where
I never know; but once in each year, lightening
My weary path.   Mysterious and strange,
Thou ne'er before hast spoken.   Thou blameless Catharine,
Return.   Our sins of jealousy have borne
Such fruit as grows from poisoned ground; and yet
Nor Time nor forcing Will can make us what
We were in our first wedded life.   These agents
Are far too weak; they never can restore
To us the faith that's lost in our past lives, —
Lost like a pearl dropped in dissolving flame,
Its white and saintly fabric gone in a moment.
Unhappy Catharine, and thou my more
Unhappy self!   These revels mock us.   Poor mask!

[Lays down his mask.

The mask that hath been torn from off my heart

This night hath left a shadow tenfold darker
Than is thine own.   I'll go seek Violet,
For she is like the beauteous sunlit day.
              [*Listening to strains of music from the ball-room.*
Music doth hold melodious discourse.
                   [*Walks, in meditation and soliloquy.*
Why, I am growing melancholy.   My sun's
Across the line and courses the horizon;
My nights are growing longer than my days;
The glad days wane, until, as in the deepening
Winter, near the northern pole, they'll come
But for a moment, a wedge of light between
Two nights.   Oh, hasten, come, thou blank, perpetual
Night!   [*Music ceases.*]   The instruments are dumb, the
    players
Are at rest; but their unceased vibrations
On struggling chords yet tremble in my breast.
Alas! such is the growth of melancholy.
                              [*Exit.*

Act the Fourth.

SCENE I. — *A room at the Dolphin Inn. Guns, pistols, swords, and other weapons scattered around.* WHETSTONE *in armor, lying upon a sofa, disquietly sleeping.*

Enter BLUEGRASS *carrying a large dictionary.*

BLUEGRASS.

He sleeps. 'T is well. For centuries men, with eager eyes fixed upon the horizon, have awaited the coming of the purely literary duel. The auspicious morn is about to dawn, in fact, to bloom upon this magnificent star of ours, when, in affairs of honor, bloody swords, odious gunpowder, and slaughtering bullets no longer shall disgrace the planet.

WHETSTONE [*dreaming*].

Take away the sword ! Do not say I killed you !

BLUEGRASS.

He dreams of the combat. Rest, warrior, rest ! Safe within this volume, and at your timely service, are such dire missiles, fearful and momentous cartridges, bombs, shells, fowling-pieces, blunderbusses, mortars, and battering-rams, as have rent nations asunder and awed the world. Can base gunpowder and lead do so much ? O puissant volume,

116

armory and magazine, I will select from your mighty stores, for my principal's sake, weapons which shall strike terror and dismay to his adversary's heart. Yes, a full dozen of as bold bad words as were ever conned from out thy depths by a dyspeptic writer at midnight hour in editorial den.

[A rooster crows.

WHETSTONE [*still dreaming*].

See how he glares upon me!

BLUEGRASS.

Rest, warrior, rest! You go forth not to death, but to glorious immortality. *[Rooster crows.*

WHETSTONE [*starting up*].

Take him away; he is killing me! Oh, oh! [*Observing* BLUEGRASS] Who are you?

BLUEGRASS [*cheerfully*].

Your trusty friend and second in this valiant enterprise. I've just returned from Fopdoodle's second. We have arranged the place, time, weapons, and conditions of the duel very satisfactorily.

WHETSTONE.

You seem to enjoy it!

BLUEGRASS.

Listen, and you'll enjoy it too.

117

WHETSTONE.

Let me know the worst.

BLUEGRASS.

Place, the little clearing in the darkened wood behind the hill.

WHETSTONE.

Why did n't you make it in the West, behind the Rocky Mountains?

BLUEGRASS.

Time, one hour before sunrise.

WHETSTONE.

Why did n't you make it next year, in the dark of the moon? Major, I feel that my blood will be upon your so-called head.

BLUEGRASS.

Not if my head can save you, and I think it can. With some acuteness, I secured Scythe as attendant surgeon, in case of an accident, and he has already gone to the spot with all his surgical implements of healing. [*Rooster crows.*

WHETSTONE.

What 's that? Is 't the signal?

BLUEGRASS.

Listen! now for the weapons.

WHETSTONE.

Don't, Major, don't!

BLUEGRASS.

With some archness in archery, I first chose crossbows as most fitting for lovers' duels, but abandoned them as too crosswise. Blunderbusses I rejected, as too blundering for us; and, noting the weakness of our enemy in diction, I at last chose dictionaries, big and unabridged, and made by the most celebrated word-smiths.

WHETSTONE.

Dictionaries! Did you say dictionaries? Major, now my anger is reviving. Now, by all that 's terrible, I 'll fight till there 's not a leaf or lid left. Why, the first blow I give him shall be a jaw-breaker. He 'll think himself smitten, like the Philistines, by a jawbone. Major, get me a diction-ary with iron clasps; but one is not enough, my boy. I 'll strike him with two dictionaries. [*Rooster crows.*

BLUEGRASS.

Erroneous hero! You are in honor bound not to deal him any blows with vulgar material-bound paper.

WHETSTONE.

How then, my boy, how then?

BLUEGRASS.

Listen to the conditions of the duel. At a distance of two

paces, you and Fopdoodle, each aided by his respective second, will each respectively select, for each fire from his inexhaustible dictionary or armory, one animal noun for his projectile, and one adjective, — for your adjective is your gunpowder to your bullet of a noun. These two, to wit: one animal noun and one adjective, each of you will form into a cartridge, or epithet, and at the word *Fire* each will fire it at his adversary.

WHETSTONE.

Bless you, my boy, we are saved! You shall always be editor of the Eagle. My boy, you must have known I did n't want to kill him. Major, stand by me to the last.

BLUEGRASS.

I 'll do it. I am a connoisseur in epithets; and your animal noun with adjective conjoined is a terrible weapon. O book, how like a poet thou art! — in pleasant moods full of balmlike words, but in anger javelined like a porcupine. Be thou a cage filled to the cover's brim with fierce animal nouns which fret their paper cage of leaves to pounce upon the enemy. Remember, at each fire call him some outrageous animal, and exploit the animal with an explosive adjective.

WHETSTONE.

I 'll do it. The gourd-headed baboon!

[*Rooster crows.*

BLUEGRASS.

Good; a very fine line shot! But don't waste your ammunition here. Wait until you get your enemy into close quarters, and meanwhile steady your nerves and tongue. Remember, no faltering of the tongue.

WHETSTONE.

How goes the night outdoors?

BLUEGRASS.

All's well! Now shall I behold the first genuine literary duel ever fought on this magnificent star of ours, while the sun trails his sanguinary banners along the eastern sky.

[Rooster crows.

WHETSTONE.

Why does he crow so often?

BLUEGRASS.

It is the martial bird of morn, brave chanticleer — the vocal lighthouse of the dawn. Six times has the rooster crowed. [*Rooster again crows.*] And yet again he crows, — seven times, mysterious number! With crimson comb and whetted spurs, he sniffs this duel from his lofty perch in the heavenly balcony.

WHETSTONE.

How says the time?

BLUEGRASS.

It lacks but little of the hour. We'll prove no laggards

on the field of honor. Come on. Make haste! Away, away, or we'll be late to join the fray! We'll get our lanterns on the way. [*Rooster crows.*] [*Exeunt.*

SCENE II. — *A clearing in a wood.* SCYTHE, *with lantern, arranging surgical instruments.*

Enter, running, FOPDOODLE, *attended by* TOM, *his valet and second, carrying lantern and dictionary.*

FOPDOODLE.

What man is this?

TOM.

Good master, this is the attendant surgeon, agreed upon by Whetstone's second and myself, your own second and humble valet.

FOPDOODLE.

Kind Mr. Surgeon, if we two fall at once, save me first; and I promise you a great reward from father's patrimony. And as our wounds we do refer to you, I move to make you referee. Kind Mr. Surgeon, prescribe for me a breathing spell. [SCYTHE *examines him with glass.*] Tom, my man, stand firm! For as we crossed through yonder green and peaceful field, by some ominous mischance a sleeping, low-bred, fiery bull arose, with eyes big as our lanterns, filled with the flaming fat of animal fury. He chased; and as we fled, I thought I was pursued by an infuriated animal noun. Oh, doctor, prescribe for me a breathing spell.

TOM.

Good master, here is your dictionary, if you'd take a breathing spell.

FOPDOODLE.

Unlettered ruffian, uncompassionate fool, do I clothe and fee you for this? Hand me my spirit of hartshorn to brace my spirits up. [*Using smelling-bottle.*] Had I but had this spirit of hartshorn in my nostrils, I would have had the spirit to face a thousand bulls. Where's the infuriated dictionary?

TOM.

Here it is, good master.

FOPDOODLE.

Turn to the fearful B's; I know some good shots in the B's.

TOM.

Here they are, good master.

FOPDOODLE.

Do we yet espy the foe?

SCYTHE [*looking through glass*].

I see him coming over the brow of the hill, and he'll be here in a wink.

FOPDOODLE.

Alas, if I should fall !

TOM.

I'll raise you up again.

FOPDOODLE.

Base horizontal knave, thou canst again raise up my body, but not my character.

Enter WHETSTONE *and* BLUEGRASS, *with lantern and dictionary.*

BLUEGRASS.

A brave salutation, gentlemen! We will pursue the code of honor where it does not conflict with us. Let the principals advance, and shake hands in the usual way, to show that they in humor and honor are not ill. [WHET-STONE *and* FOPDOODLE *advance and shake hands. To* TOM] We must compare size, weight, and calibre of type. [*They compare dictionaries.*] The weapons are of the same edition. Now for choice of positions; but there are two esteemed objects in the heavens, — Mars and the moon; for them we'll toss up. [*To* TOM] Head or tail? [*Tosses up a coin.*]

TOM.

Tail.

BLUEGRASS.

Head it is. I've won! I place Fopdoodle with the moon in his face, and Whetstone with the planet Mars at his back. [*Measures off two paces and places the principals.*] In affairs of honor, delay is a vice, despatch a virtue. I propose, between each fire, thirty seconds for loading, that after the words, One, two, — fire! each one shall fire, and that this continue until one be prostrated; also that Surgeon Scythe give the word and be referee. But we'll try to preserve a gentlemanly harmony.

TOM.

We agree.

[*Each second supports his principal, and* SCYTHE *times them with his watch.*

FOPDOODLE.

Tom, my man, turn to the C's; I know a terrible animal noun in the C's.

BLUEGRASS.

Here, Mayor Whetstone, is your adjective for gunpowder, — Patagonian.

WHETSTONE.

I'll take bat for a bullet.

BLUEGRASS.

Now, by the planet Mars, you have chosen the most unearthly bullet in the whole menagerie of animal nouns.

FOPDOODLE [*to* TOM].

I've got it. I now turn to U for my gunpowder.

TOM.

Master, I have no gunpowder.

125

The Merchant Prince

FOPDOODLE.

You unlettered utensil, you! The letter **U**.

SCYTHE.

Time! One, two, — fire!

WHETSTONE.

Patagonian bat!

FOPDOODLE [*pronouncing calf with broad sound of letter* a].
Unutterable calf!

BLUEGRASS.

A foul! a foul! I claim a foul.

SCYTHE.

Upon what do you base your foul?

BLUEGRASS.

Upon the letter *a* in calf. In place of rightly firing calf
with the Italian sound of *a*, as in bah, he wrongly fired calf
with *a* broad. Therefore he fired *a* broadside, with sound the
same as in ball. I claim the foul is sound.

SCYTHE.

Let me examine your weapon [*examining* FOPDOODLE's
dictionary]. I plainly see a calf with two little dots like bud-
ding horns above the letter *a*, denoting the Italian sound;
and as you wrongfully fired broad *a*, and as broad *a* in your

weapon is denoted by two little dots below the *a*, I rule you struck below the belt, and hence *a* foul.

BLUEGRASS.

First foul for Fopdoodle.

WHETSTONE [*aside*].

See him tremble.

FOPDOODLE [*aside*].

I struck him badly.

SCYTHE.

Gentlemen, are your honors satisfied?

WHETSTONE.

Never! War to the word knife!

FOPDOODLE.

Never! War to the word hilt!

SCYTHE.

Then sadly be it said: Reload. I'll see if there is any blood on yonder red and warlike Mars. [*Looks at Mars with glass, while the others reload from dictionaries.*] Time! One, two, — fire!

FOPDOODLE.

Hyperborean ibex!

WHETSTONE.

Parabolical goose !

SCYTHE.

Are you satisfied ?

FOPDOODLE.

Never !   War to the word knife !

WHETSTONE.

Never !   War to the word hilt !

SCYTHE.

Reload.   [*They reload.*]   Time !   One, two, — fire !

FOPDOODLE.

Impecunious porcupine !

WHETSTONE.

Hypothecated buzzard !

   [*Lightning and thunder, while* SCYTHE *examines the sky
      with glass.*

FOPDOODLE.

Listen, Tom !   I think I hear the police !   The police !
Let us be going !

BLUEGRASS.

Hold !   'T is but the thunder, heaven's police drilling
near the distant horizon.   Let their lanterns flash and their
clubs smash the sky, but this duel shall go on.

Scythe.

Gentlemen, reload. [*They reload.*] Time! One, two, —

Fopdoodle.

Hold! My tongue slipped.

Tom.

And the lightning 's blown my lantern out.

[*Lightning and thunder.*

Bluegrass [*re-lighting* Tom's *lantern*].

I hope I may re-light your lantern without an explosion. A fearful storm is brewing, but we must make them fight until one falls.

Tom.

I 'll stand by my master.

Scythe.

Time! One, two, — fire!

Whetstone.

Categorical catamount!

Fopdoodle.

Bog-trotting bull-frog!

Bluegrass.

Foul, foul, a most terrible and bulldozing foul, — a double-barrelled fowling-piece ; a two-bullet foul.

The Merchant Prince

TOM.

A bull-frog is no fowl.

BLUEGRASS.

A most naked and unfeathered fowl.

SCYTHE.

Upon what purely scientific facts do you now perch your alleged fowl?

BLUEGRASS.

Upon the rail between bull and frog. Bull-frog is a compound animal noun, composed of one bull and one frog, connected by a hyphen, or narrow ligament, like the Siamese twins, — two animals in one. I ask judgment.

[*Lightning and thunder.*

SCYTHE.

Listen to my decision; for though it should rain bullfrogs, I'll decide by analysis. The difference lies between the grammatical bull-frog and the purely animal bull-frog. Grammar does not concern the animal bull-frog, but has much to do with the word bull-frog. The purely animal bull-frog is manifestly not a fowl; but inasmuch as by the rules only one animal noun is allowed at a shot, and whereas the grammatical bull-frog is compounded of two animals linked by a hyphen, I declare them a chain-shot, disallowed in civilized warfare, and a foul of the worst description.

TOM.

Good master, he says 't is a foul.

FOPDOODLE.

We're in bad odor with this referee. I smell foul play.
Give me my spirit of hartshorn, or I faint.

TOM.

Here it is, good master.
[FOPDOODLE *smells of hartshorn, and* WHETSTONE
drinks out of a flask.

SCYTHE.

Time! One, two, — fire!

FOPDOODLE.

Humpbacked sham!

WHETSTONE.

Infamous liar!
FOPDOODLE.

You man in buckram! You rambling sham! You blue
sham, three-cornered sham, catalectic sham! You panting,
rampant sham, black sham, white sham, speckled sham!

BLUEGRASS [*to* SCYTHE].

Stop him! He has opened the menagerie. Foul, foul!
He has fired a whole sham battery.

WHETSTONE.

I'll slay him on the spot. You catacomb! you catas-
trophic, cataleptic, catacoustic cat! Pooh! you spotted

poodle, you freckled poodle, you yellow-brindled poodle! dogfish! you dogmatic-dogwood-doggerel dog.

> [*Lightning and thunder.*

TOM [*supporting* FOPDOODLE].

Good master, bear up. 'T is only a shower of cats and dogs.

FOPDOODLE [*fainting*].

Give me a drink of tiger's blood!

BLUEGRASS [*to* WHETSTONE].

See, you have struck him ; he is falling.

> [FOPDOODLE *falls, clasping his dictionary.*

SCYTHE [*to* TOM].

Run quickly. Catch me a sheep in yonder field. By transfusing blood from its veins to his, I'll make the weak brave, the faint alive. [*Taking up a surgical instrument.*] Now, great Science, help me!

TOM.

Good master, I go to get the sheep. [*Exit* TOM.

BLUEGRASS.

Long live and let live the literary duel!

> [*Lightning and thunder. The scene closes while* WHET-
> STONE, BLUEGRASS, *and* SCYTHE *gather around*
> FOPDOODLE, *administering to him.*

SCENE III. — *The Glen of Ferns. Midday.*

Enter IDEAL.

IDEAL.

See how great Nature lavishes in this
Hard wrinkle in the globe a subtle and
Refining power, as if it were the open
Volume of the earth with fern-clad cliffs
For lettered pages.   Here the glad sun comes
In his most favoring hour, with impress of
A God, in splendor sparkling down the glen.
Ye ferns that spring along these cliffs with light
And airy grace, see but my Violet,
And ye shall take a new and tender charm.
Yon rainbow, in the sportive mist above
The cascade glowing, well a brighter bow
Might grow when it doth catch the arch words of
Bright Violet.   Ye berries crimsoning
On yonder bushes, were ye roseate
As are the ripe red lips of Violet,
Wise men a holiday would take, and go
A-berrying.   E'en weeds along the cliff
Were like some pretty fault in Violet, —
Sweet contrast growing but for beauty's foil.
Be free and happy, all created things ;
Ye singing birds, your melodies attune ;
And ye, blithe squirrels— Peeping Toms of trees —

The Merchant Prince

From out your leafy coverts peep, and I'll
Not jealous be.

Enter VIOLET, *at top of rustic stairway.*

Ay, there she comes, fair Violet!

VIOLET.

Heigh-ho! Why art thou down so low?

IDEAL.

That I may upward gaze at thee. For as
One in the deep bottom of a well, above
May see a star at midday, so do I
See thee from the deep bottom of this glen.

VIOLET.

With fancy thou dost blithely scale this stair,
As doth some heavenly singer; yet thou seest
Thou art still at the bottom of the glen.

IDEAL.

Let us be like two notes in music blent;
Thou high, I low; yet both in sweet accord.

VIOLET.

Truly, thou art my Ideal. But, alack!
I've called thee by thy name.

IDEAL.

Give thou it me, and I will bear no other.

of Cornville.

VIOLET.

Thou hadst it long ago.

IDEAL.

To be thy Ideal more real were
Than to achieve all other reals.

VIOLET [*archly*].

Alas! the hard vicissitudes of life!

IDEAL.

Why, how now, Violet? I'll bear them all.

VIOLET.

All hard vicissitudes?

IDEAL.

All.

VIOLET.

I have an uncle.

IDEAL.

If he's a hard vicissitude, I'll bear him too.

VIOLET.

I'll go tell my uncle. [*Going.*]

IDEAL.

Nay, hold. Within thy words, as in the cinctured
Filaments of lace thou wear'st, I see the fine
Transparent tracery of gossamer
Designs. In such a web I'd fain be caught.

The Merchant Prince

Violet.

And I 'd fain catch thee.

Ideal.

Come, let us walk within this pleasant glen;
And if we weary, — on a mossy bank,
In the cool shade of interlacing leaves, —
We 'll watch the gentle coquetry between
A burning sunbeam and a shaded fern.
There 's not a fern-leaf, berry, blade of grass,
Nor flower, but I 'll gather it for thee.
If at thy feet it grow, then I 'll kneel there;
If higher, in a crevice of the cliff,
Together we will reach for it, and in
The touching of our finger-tips it shall
Part company with earth in ecstasy.
And if, above, thou dost but gladly view
That most sky-kissing flower, the heavenly bluebell,
Which with transparent hue embellishes
The summit of the cliff, why, I 'll climb there.

Violet.

And leave me in the lone recesses of the glen?

Ideal.

If thou didst not detain me with thine eyes;
For if, in climbing upward, I looked back,
I 'd see the sky and bluebell in thine eyes,
And so return to thee.   Come, Violet, come.

VIOLET.

Ah, me!   See what a deep, deep stair it is.
[*Aside*] Aloof the bluebell, lovers joy to see.
[*Aloud*] I 'll not descend.

IDEAL.

Then I 'll invoke
The spirit of this lovely glen, that dwells
In yonder rock, to aid in my petition.
     [*Turns and calls to rock on further side of glen.*
Come, Violet!
     [*An echo is heard repeating* VIOLET.

VIOLET.

I think I hear my uncle calling;
I must go.   Adieu!

IDEAL.

Think not so.   I but now called Violet,
And what thou heard'st was the far echo of
Thy name, that 's borne by yonder rock from out
This cheering vale to listening hills beyond.
It is a wanton, merry rock that doth
Delight to sweetly hold discourse in doubling
Of thy name.   But as it hath no beard
Upon its face, except a fringe of ferns,
I 'll not be jealous.   For such gentle service,
Violet, give not the rock the hardness
Of thy uncle's heart; but stay.

The Merchant Prince

VIOLET.

Between thee and the rock, I almost am persuaded.

IDEAL.

Sweet Violet, do not go, — be persuaded
Altogether ; for although this is
A sheltered glen, with pleasant sunshine tempered,
Yet from thy coldness I would perish as
A homeless midnight traveller, embedded
'Mid bewildering snowbanks.

VIOLET.

Say not so ; for if thou, my dear Ideal,
On such a cruel, frosty bank lay dying,
And I were Violet beneath the snow,
As violets do often grow, I 'd call
On all the powers in stars above and in
The earth below to move the frosty barrier.
I 'll come to thee.

>   [*The scene closes while* VIOLET *descends the stair, and*
>   IDEAL *advances to meet her.*

of Cornville.

Act the Fifth.

SCENE I. — *A room at the Dolphin Inn.* *Evening.*

Enter WHETSTONE *with* BLUEGRASS *in black dress as his shadow.* *Each with guitar and song-book.*

BLUEGRASS.

A day and night, — and now another day hath waned for our recuperation ; and our adventures have flown on lightning wings to Cornville. Now do we start on new emprise.

WHETSTONE.

Major Bluegrass, this serenade must be played on the hard-pan. Put me through to-night, and I 'll make you half-owner of the Cornville Eagle.

BLUEGRASS.

Trust me, I 'll be your musical secretary ! With the Eagle and Ninon, I could soar through life like a bird.

WHETSTONE.

And I 'll soar with Violet. Why, hello ! I 've forgotten all about Susan. Where 'll I leave Susan ?

139

BLUEGRASS.

Susan! Your housekeeper! Why, what takes you back to Cornville at such a sky-crisis as this? The great point in a flight of romance is never to approach earth. Susan! Why, Susan will tarry here below and superintend the cuisine, so that you and Violet may have a warm repast when you come down from your sky-parlor.

WHETSTONE.

I wonder what Susan will say when I bring home my bride.

BLUEGRASS.

As one good man should say to another, first bridle your bride.

WHETSTONE.

Why, Major, Susan and I were young together, and we loved, or thought we did. She wanted to marry, I wanted to wait; consequence, compromise. I engaged her as my housekeeper. There's romance for you!

BLUEGRASS.

'T is an ancient parallel.

WHETSTONE.

In our serenade, what shall I do?

BLUEGRASS.

The guitar you hold you cannot play; hence I'll do the mechanical upon the strings, while you twit the circumambient air from the bridge musical of your instrument. And if you 'd prove me with a double burden, I 'll bear both words and music ; in which event you 'll give the color and visible gesture of description. Stand you beneath some close-leaved tree, where the night overlaps, and I 'll be concealed near you in the shrubbery. Later, I 'll emerge behind you, as your true shadow.

WHETSTONE.

All right, I 'll give the motions. Now, let 's see what we have in the song-book. [*Opening song-book.*] Here 's the Midnight S renade ; and Beauteous Lady I Adore Thee. That 's business. Here 's a whole grist of meeting songs : [*reading*] Meet Me at the Lane ; Meet Me by Moonlight ; Meet Me, Darling, in the Dell ; Meet Me down by the Sea ; Meet Me in the Arbor ; Meet Me in the Twilight. Where 'll this end ? Meet Me 'neath the Slippery-Elm Tree. Meet Me in the Willow-Glen. Why, Major, the earth is covered with meeting-places. But wait ! [*Examining book and pondering.*] What book-carpenter did this work ? Here's Black-Eyed Susan —[*aside*] Susan has brown eyes — [*aloud*] sandwiched between Paddle your own Canoe and the Pirates' Chorus.

BLUEGRASS.

He was a ship-carpenter who did his work ship-shape.

WHETSTONE [*reading*].

Comin' thro' the Rye, Comin' thro' the Rye, — that

sounds homelike. Major, my boy, sing and play while I act it.

> BLUEGRASS *sings and plays Comin' thro' the Rye, while* WHETSTONE *accompanies with pantomime.*

BLUEGRASS.

Demosthenes the Athenian, being interrogated, replied that action makes the orator. I may add that it makes the singer.

WHETSTONE.

You 're right. [*Examining song-book.*] Here 's a whole nest of love-songs: Love, Beautiful Love; Love in a Cottage; Love Launched a Ferry-boat.

BLUEGRASS.

'T is not ferry-boat, but fairy boat.

WHETSTONE [*reading*].

Love is at the Helm.

BLUEGRASS.

That 's when love 's at sea.

WHETSTONE [*reading*].

Love is like the Morning Dew.

BLUEGRASS.

We 're approaching land again.

WHETSTONE [*reading*].

Love's Perfect Cure.

BLUEGRASS.

We don't need it.

WHETSTONE [*reading*].

Love's the Greatest Plague.

BLUEGRASS.

Hold on! yes, we do.

WHETSTONE [*reading*].

Love Me Little, Love Me Long; Love, Love, oh, what is Love? Major, my boy, that settles it. We must find out. Hurrah! I feel like a new man! Let's be going! If I fail, Northlake shall not have a dollar. Violet's the only collateral he can put up. If I don't get her, I'll take the next train to Cornville and marry Susan on the spot. She's been a good housekeeper to me these many years; and once when I was sick she bathed my feet in hot water and mustard, and put a hot flannel around — I think it was my throat; and her elder-blossom tea can't be beaten.

BLUEGRASS.

Do you falter?

WHETSTONE.

No; I'll have what I want. You remember the bay

colt that cost me five thousand dollars? People thought I was a fool, but I was n't.

BLUEGRASS.

You were a horse diplomat.

WHETSTONE.

Exactly. I saw points, and now the colt has a great record. I see points about that girl Violet that no one else sees. She's an extraordinary girl, a thoroughbred, and I'll back my judgment with my money.

BLUEGRASS.

What if she don't take kindly to you?

WHETSTONE.

Watch me closely, and you'll see me win her to-night. What's the use of money, if you can't get — points, my boy, when you want them? And yet —

BLUEGRASS.

And yet what?

WHETSTONE.

And yet Susan has points too. She can roast a goose splendidly, — and that elder-blossom tea! But enough of this. Away to serenade.

[*Exeunt.*

# of Cornville.

POMPEY [*merrily*].

Yah! yah! I say, Hannibal, Lake Shore's g'wone up. I make pile money on dat happy shore, shure. Stocks am de ting to put de money in de stockin'.

HANNIBAL [*gloomily*].

So! so! I lose pile money on dat Hudson Ribber. My banker telegram fo' moh margin every fifteen minutes fo' foh hours. De agony of dem hours I can nebber tell you, Pompey. De telegram-wire, and de tongue of lightnin', holler, Moh margin! Hudson Ribber g'wone down, — moh margin! I and de ole woman scrape and scrape, and empty de big stockin' bank dat de old woman hab under de bed fo' de rainy day; still it holler, Moh margin! And den de old woman raise de washtub 'gainst her lawful husband. I nebber tink dat ribber railroad could sink so fast. Pompey, it am de fashion to condumdole wid your misfortunate neighbor; how much you condumdole wid me, Pompey?

POMPEY.

You hear me, chile! I lose moh money on dat Hudson Ribber dan you ebber see.

HANNIBAL.

Why, honey, how am dat? You hab no Hudson Ribber stock.

The Merchant Prince

I was g'wone down de ribber on de canal-boat, when I losed it. Yah, yah!

HANNIBAL.

Pompey, you am too friv'lous and vis'nary fo' de bus'ness man, — fo' de stock op'rator.

POMPEY.

Hannibal, I hab de call on you. Now let us confabulate togedder like sensible people. Ober two hours ago, I see de mess'nger boy bring de telegram. It ware from Mr. Northlake's banker, and it read: You made five hundred thousand dollars to-day on Lake Shore stock. Now you hab seen Mr. Northlake cast down, way down, — tremendously, moh dan usual, fo' 'bout a month, — way down, 'cause he lose all his own and Miss Violet's fortune speculatin', — way down; but when he read dat, he smile like de little chile; and he say to me: Pompey, dere 'll be a surprise-party yere to-night. Spread de banquet fo' de guests. And now we doin' it, ain't we?

HANNIBAL.

I'm glad ob dat, fo' Miss Violet's sake, and de tings she gibs me; but dis am de point I must determinate before de limbs work easy: Ware am de margin g'wone dat I don't hab, — de one thousand seven hundred and ninety-seven cents?

POMPEY.

Dat, chile, am g'wone ware de weasel 's g'wone wid de egg.

of Cornville.

HANNIBAL.

Dat am a big weasel to get away wid one thousand seven hundred and ninety-seven cents. I'll write my banker, shure, in de mornin' 'bout de wrong p'ints he gibs me. Dat's my p'intin' 'pinion 'bout him. Maybe he'll loan me it back again, — dat one thousand seven hundred and ninety-seven cents. [*Exeunt.*

SCENE III. — *The lawn in front of* NORTHLAKE'S *Villa.*

Enter WHETSTONE *and* BLUEGRASS, *with guitars, stealthily advancing through the shrubbery, and appearing upon the lawn.*

BLUEGRASS.

Now do we stand upon the green lawn of fresh enterprise. Stand yourself 'neath yonder tree, and fix your eyes on the balcony [WHETSTONE *takes position accordingly*], while I, from behind this green projecting wing of shrubbery, project our ripening song [*moving behind the shrubbery*]. First, our song of salutation, with fresh words.

BLUEGRASS, *under cover of the shrubbery, sings and plays, while* WHETSTONE *accompanies with pantomime.*

The moon is on the hills,
    The glow-worm's in the grass;
The nightingales have bills,
    The owls have singing-class.

147

The Merchant Prince

BLUEGRASS *ceases singing while* WHETSTONE *continues pantomime.*

WHETSTONE.

Give me more words!

BLUEGRASS.

I 've forgotten the rest, and therefore take a rest.

WHETSTONE.

Look! the door is opening. [*Door partly opens, and* POMPEY *shows his head.*] Great thunder — a black walnut!

BLUEGRASS.

Vanish, thou black January! [POMPEY *vanishes.*] We 'll strike a mellower melody, and yonder balcony shall bear fruitage brighter than October. The prize of the troubadours in the courts of love was the golden violet.

WHETSTONE.

Give me no more sentimental nonsense. Sing a song of business.

BLUEGRASS.

That 's clever. I feel the inspiration. I 'll improvise a matter-of-fact descriptive ballad illustrating the moral maxim, Business before love.

148

BLUEGRASS sings and plays; WHETSTONE accompanies with pantomime, and joins in singing last line of each stanza.

Katie and Jack got up at morn,
And she came with two ears of corn,
And he came with his brassy horn,
　To drive the ducks to market, O!

Now Katie's ducks were white as snow,
But Jackie's ducks were black as crow;
So o'er the hills away they go,
　Driving the ducks to market, O!

Then Jackie blew his brassy horn,
And Katie shelled her ears of corn,
While the rooster crowed upon the thorn,
　Driving the ducks to market, O!

Now Katie loved, and so did he,
And he his horn hung on a tree;
Oh, they were glad as the busy bee,
　Keeping the ducks from market, O!

The moon fell down behind a hill;
The sun winked at the miller's mill;
The lark got up upon his quill,
　Keeping the ducks from market, O!

Alas! alas! green grew the grass,
The duckies, hunting garden sass,
Fell in a trap. Alas! alas!
　Keeping the ducks from market, O!

The Merchant Prince

Then he cried chuckie, duckie, O !
Then she cried duckie, chuckie, O !
But oh, alas ! it was no go,
    Driving the ducks to market, O !

MORAL.

The moral's plain as the bumble-bee,
Clear on the top of a tall tree.
Oh, wait ! if lovers you may be ;
    First drive your ducks to market, O !

Enter VIOLET *upon the balcony.*

VIOLET.

I plainly see there's business in this night. [*Perceiving*
WHETSTONE.] Why, 't is the self-same knight that did
bedight another night, but far more musical. There's a sad
want of unity here, as no music, however rich, can me unite
to yonder knight. [*Addressing* WHETSTONE.] Do my two
eyes behold that Mayor Whetstone, of Cornville, near the
capital of Illinois, called Hercules after his grand-uncle
Hercules, who drove the Indians down the Mississippi ?

WHETSTONE.

You do behold with two, unless with one you kindly wink
upon me, which I half believe you do.

VIOLET.

Is thy meaning double or single ?

WHETSTONE.

Sweet Miss Violet, I have been a man with an eye single to business, but who would double his business.

BLUEGRASS.

Don't give her any quandaries.

VIOLET.

Why, thou hast changed thy voice!

WHETSTONE [*aside*].

Major, you rascal, assume my voice!

BLUEGRASS [*assuming* WHETSTONE'S *voice*].

Sweet Violet, it is the air, that's sometimes tuneful and sometimes not, that doth effect the change.

VIOLET.

Thou art an artful man.

BLUEGRASS [*assuming* WHETSTONE'S *voice*].

Sweet Violet, 't is even noted so.

WHETSTONE [*aside*].

Confound you, 't is not so!

BLUEGRASS [*assuming* WHETSTONE'S *voice*].

I meant to say the air is so.

The Merchant Prince

Violet.

If thou sowest the air with so, so, thy harvest will be no, no. The air upon this balcony well balances its fruitage.

Whetstone [aside].

You villain, we're caught!

Violet.

I'll not complain if thou wilt sing me another song.

Whetstone [aside].

Major, you rascal, another song!

Bluegrass [aside].

I don't know any more.

Whetstone [kneeling].

Sweet Miss Violet, upon this green grass I vow to love you as long as grass grows. Oh, Miss Violet, you're too young to know what you may lose. You may lose the real Merchant Prince of Cornville, near the capital of Illinois, called Hercules after his grand-uncle Hercules, who drove the real Indians reeling down the real Mississippi.

Violet.

Rise, thou mighty chief of merchandise. I set much store by thee.

Whetstone [rising and aside].

Major, my boy, did you hear that?

VIOLET.

Great Prince, it is my humor to be enamoured of thy union of business and romance. [*Calls to* NINON *within.* NINON *enters.* BLUEGRASS *leaves the shrubbery and goes behind* WHETSTONE, *as his shadow.*] Take no leaves from my shrubbery. What is 't that 's back of thee, Prince ?

WHETSTONE.

'T is but the shadow cast from me by the moonlight.

VIOLET.

The tree 'neath which thou standest is cedrine, and its laced boughs, filtering the moonlight, cast an interlacing shadow on the lawn ; upon this plot, now, in part, a deeper shadow rests, like shadow upon shadow.

BLUEGRASS [*sings in recitative, and* WHETSTONE *accompanies with pantomime*].

'T is but a shadow, 't is but a shadow cast from me by the moonlight.

NINON.

I hear ze voice of ze shadow, ze pretty shadow. Oh, zat I had ze shadow up on ze balcony ! Charmant !

VIOLET.

Fie, Ninon, what wouldst thou with the fleeting shadow of this Merchant Prince ? Thou hadst not even the shadow of sentiment.

153

The Merchant Prince

NINON.

Dear mistress, I see ze rainbow in ze shadow.   Superbe!

BLUEGRASS [*aside*].

I 've been too long a shadow.

WHETSTONE [*aside*].

You rascal, make yourself shorter!

BLUEGRASS.

Black slave that I am, thus to serve this merchant prince of merchandise!

WHETSTONE.

I 'm a solid man, and my shadow lies solid.

NINON.

Poor shadow, come off ze cold, cold ground!

BLUEGRASS [*sings in recitative, and* WHETSTONE *accompanies with pantomime*].

The shadow is slave to the substance. Who can separate them? None. Who can separate them? None, — none but Ninon.

VIOLET.

Ninon, 't is marvellously good, — but we must go. [*Slowly going.*] Good-night alike to substance and shadow. Yet, stay! [*Advancing.*] Didst ever study arithmetic?

BLUEGRASS [*sings in recitative, and* WHETSTONE *accompanies with pantomime*].

Addition I have at my finger-tips. [*Counting notes upon his guitar.*] One, two, three, four, five. Multiplication I have by heart.

WHETSTONE [*aside*].

Throw in all the multiplication-table.

BLUEGRASS [*sings in recitative, and* WHETSTONE *accompanies with pantomime*].

Come, come, let us learn, let us sing. Come, come, let us learn the multiplication-table. Come, let us sing the multiplication-table.

VIOLET.

Thou art too multitudinous, and wert born for the opera; yet I will give thee a problem that thou shalt solve, not with thy digits, but with thy pedals. I will teach thee subtraction, and separate thy shadow from thy substance by plane trigonometry.

WHETSTONE [*aside*].

Major, steady! Listen for the click of the trigger.

VIOLET.

A triangle is a sweet instrument in the mathematics of love; for oft, about the first of April nights, I've watched the merry wild geese in the sky flying northward in musical and far-sounding triangles.

155

WHETSTONE.

I know them well. I have one in my brass band in Cornville.

VIOLET.

And yet triangulation by moonlight were a pleasant death, betwixt substance and shadow. Ninon, girl, quick! bring me my bronze-covered trigonometry. [*Exit* NINON.

WHETSTONE.

Hold on! There must be some mistake here. Please don't pull any trigger on us!

BLUEGRASS [*aside*].

And make angels of us!

WHETSTONE.

Hold on, Miss Violet! I don't want to be an angel yet.

VIOLET.

There's no fairer weapon than a book, and I'll make no angel of thee,

BLUEGRASS [*aside*].

Let's cap the climax and capitulate.

Re-enter NINON, *with book.*

NINON.

Mistress Violet, here is ze book.

# of Cornville.

VIOLET.

I do not need it now. My memory serves me as well.
Prince, fear not; trigonometry is a peaceful art that maids
may practice, and thou beneath my patient yoke shalt help
me draw this triangle. One side thereof shall be betwixt
thy stationed shadow and myself, another 'twixt thy shadow
and thyself, and the base side thereof shall be the distance
'twixt thee and me, — whose baseness shall increase if it
decrease.   [*Pauses.*

NINON.

Kind mistress, wilt thou have ze book?

VIOLET.

No book can help me. Now do I pause [*pausing*], for in
this triangle one angle is obtuse and two acute; but my
good angel shall help me. 'T is better to be right than be
acute; therefore it shall be a right-angled triangle. [*To*
WHETSTONE.] Hence move you backward in the light.
[WHETSTONE *moves backward.*] But also from your right.
[*He moves from his right.*] Ninon, girl, see, the shadow
doth not follow!

BLUEGRASS.

Now from this angle do I see my angel.

NINON.

I know ze shadow, ze rainbow, ze major, ze grand lover!
157

The Merchant Prince

VIOLET [*to* WHETSTONE, *who has moved until he forms a right angle with* BLUEGRASS *and* VIOLET].

Move no further. Thy shadow keeps no pace with thee, and fear might well oppress a wondering maid less mathematical. Ninon, take and reflect upon yon shadow. 'T is thy sum total, and a happy one.

Enter FOPDOODLE.

FOPDOODLE.

Dear Miss Violet, I 'm cured. The sheep's blood is all out of me. Pa says I may bring you home with me; and Ma says I am a lamb with a golden fleece, but I must not alarm them by bleating — ba-bah. I have been badly off — but I assure you I am shorn of my malady. There is no longer any impediment of speech to our happiness. Oh, how I want to be a noble husband! Dear Miss Violet, may I, may I address you up so high, and I down so low? May I? May I?

VIOLET.

Thou hast too many Mays in thy calendar, but thou mayst have a cold March ere thou comest to a timely May.

FOPDOODLE.

Star of Violet, come down to the earth. No, no. O earth of black, go up to the star of Violet. Yes, yes; but the earth can't do it. What the deuce is the proper thing? Well, well —

# of Cornville.

VIOLET.

Thy question lies at bottom of a well too deep for a maid to fathom, looking down from a balcony.

FOPDOODLE.

Dear Miss Violet, may I come up?

VIOLET.

Thy ardor is alarming!

FOPDOODLE.

Dear Miss Violet, my servant, Tom, has a ladder waiting for me, and I will climb to thee. Don't be alarmed; I am harmless, O dazzling Violet!

VIOLET.

Lovers should have in their hearts ladders of words better than any made with hands. Where is thy ladder?

FOPDOODLE.

[*Calling to* TOM, *around the corner*] Tom, my man, bring your master love's ladder.

TOM.

Good master, I come.
　　[TOM *enters with a ladder and sets it against the wall.*

FOPDOODLE.

Don't let it slip! Tom, my man, stand firm. [*He ascends.*
159

The Merchant Prince

Tom.

I obey, good master.

Bluegrass [*sings in recitative and plays*].

See! see! the bold burglar. Help! help! He ascends! he ascends!

Fopdoodle [*halting*].

I — I — I, Augustus Fopdoodle, a bad burglar man! I—I, the son of my father, Fopdoodle! Pray, sweet Miss Violet, who are those rude, bad men?

Bluegrass [*sings in recitative and plays*].

We are a triangle, and we'll make a parallelogram of you. We are — we are — an accurate right-angled triangle, and we'll make, we'll make, a p-a-r — par, a-l — paral, l-e-l — parallel, o — parallelo, g-r-a-m — parallelogram — of you.

Whetstone.

Get down off the ladder!

Fopdoodle.

'T is the voice of the barbarian, Whetstone, — my animal noun, my enemy!

Enter Jack.

Jack [*to* Fopdoodle].

Put the ladder back in the garden!

FOPDOODLE.

Help me, good Jack!
> [JACK *takes hold of ladder*, *and* FOPDOODLE *tumbles from it.*

FOPDOODLE [*rising*].

O dazzling Violet, my heart's in ruins, and I'm turned down.
> [FOPDOODLE, JACK, *and* TOM *move a short distance with ladder ; when* TOM *holds*, *and* FOPDOODLE *leans upon it.*

Enter SCYTHE, *observing no one, and with hand-net, in pursuit of a night-beetle buzzing in the air.*

SCYTHE.

Where flies the beetle, I pursue.   There, I hear it now!
[*The buzz of a flying beetle is heard.*]   Lovely night-beetle!
Now you rise, and now you sink in curving flight.   [*He pursues, listening, till the sound ceases.*]   Now you've rested on a night-blooming flower, and I'll approach more softly than lover does a dreaming maid, nor wake with rude-paced step your finer sense of airy motion.   [*He advances cautiously in search.*]

VIOLET.

See, Ninon; he sees no one.   In our time let maids be jealous.   Science has its votaries as deeply rapt as love's suitors.

The Merchant Prince

SCYTHE [*stopping, and observing the beetle on a flower*].

What a rare and beautiful specimen for the Academy!
Since early eve I've followed in the moonlight, through
gardens, groves, and lawns. Now I'll capture thee. [*He
throws his net over the flower, but the beetle, escaping, flies away
with a buzzing sound, while he watches its course through his
glass.*] 'Tis a peerless beetle, with wings of purple filigreed
with gold and silver, which leave in sparkling flight a trail
of light. I'll follow it till morning, but I'll capture it.

[*Exit* SCYTHE *in pursuit, and without having observed any one.*

VIOLET.

Alack! few lovers are so ardent in their pursuit, and some
do lag most grievously. [*To* NINON] One was to come
to-night, beneath my window, whom I've yet not seen.

NINON.

But see, my mistress, something is coming up ze orchard
path.

VIOLET [*intently observing*].

'Tis distant, and yet 'tis bigger than a man's hand.
Why, Ninon, 'tis a man. How near wouldst thou say he
is?

NINON.

Courage, my mistress! he has ze fleet pace of ze
lover.

Enter IDEAL.

IDEAL.

Dear Violet, in hastening by the orchard path to meet thee 'neath thy window, I was detained by thy sweet sisters of the field, which sprang along my path in myriad gayety, while I in blissful fantasy did win them ; and here, accompanied with my love, I tender thee this bunch of golden-hearted violets.

VIOLET.

Why, 't is my Ideal! I'll ne'er forsake thee ; for were I to forsake my Ideal, that which were forsaken were better than that which were taken. To thee I'll swift descend, and, descending, I'll ascend. [*Exit* VIOLET.

NIXON [*following*].

And I'll descend to ze grand Major, for ze willing mistress makes ze willing maid. [*Exit* NIXON.

WHETSTONE.

Major, I'm for a flank movement. We're in the heat of battle. Let's head them off! Let us on! She's a prize! She's a thoroughbred! What points she has! See the points and angles she gave us. She's worth all! [*Enter* VIOLET *and* NIXON, *who are joined by* IDEAL *and* BLUE-GRASS.] She must not escape me ; I'll throw in the Eagle.

BLUEGRASS.

Hold! Not the Eagle.

163

The Merchant Prince

WHETSTONE.

The bank, the steeple, the stores, the Academy, my farm on Pearl Creek, — all, all, everything, — but I 'll have her!

NINON.

Dear Major, save ze Eagle!

BLUEGRASS.

Fear not; we 'll always share ze Eagle between us.

NINON.

Ze grand Major will not share ze Eagle, — cut ze fedders off?

BLUEGRASS.

Never, my child of innocence, never! We 'll have one sparkling hearthstone, one sprightly boudoir, one full panoplied Eagle.

NINON.

Oui, oui, très joli! charmant!

Enter NORTHLAKE *and* CATHARINE.

NORTHLAKE.

Good friends, and Mayor Whetstone, welcome all!
It is a happy and auspicious time.
This day the turn of Fortune's fickle wheel
Hath brought a double gift of joy to me.
This is my wife, from whom I was estranged, —

164

My Catharine, light of my youthful life, —
Now reunited by a tenderer tie
Than held our earlier years of wedded love.
And this same day, by sudden rise of stocks
On the Exchange, my fortune and my niece's
Have been restored to us. Swiftly hath flown
The time since when, upon a troublous day,
Yon Merchant Prince and I together planned
Without her leave, as men too oft have done,
To violate a gentle maiden's heart.
But she by maiden wit and nimble mirth
Hath warded off and foiled our ruder blows;
For Nature gives to helpless maids such powers
To guard their hearts as are undreamt of men.
Let us be glad that naught but harmless mirth
Hath been the kind result of deeper plans.
For, friends, good mirth is better than fine gold;
'T is Heaven's mercy shown to weary man,
And falls upon the heart of melancholy
As fall refreshing dews on earth at eve.
And as in sparkling drops of crystal dew
Night-clouded Earth doth clasp the light of stars,
So doth the heart of melancholy catch,
In sparkling laughter, the light of merry hearts.

WHETSTONE.

Major, now for my revenge! Send for my housekeeper,
my castle-keeper. Order Susan. I'll celebrate my nuptials
on this sea-girt strand.

The Merchant Prince

BLUEGRASS.

Shall I order the nuptial plumage?

WHETSTONE.

For both.   At once.

Enter PUNCH *with garments on each arm.*

PUNCH.

Ladies and gentlemens, I have some beautiful wedding
garments.

Enter SCYTHE, *enthusiastically, with hand-net and beetle.*

SCYTHE.

I 've caught the beetle!   [*Exhibiting a large beetle.*

WHETSTONE.

Send it to my Cornville Museum!

NORTHLAKE.

A word with thee, my gallant Mayor Whetstone:
There 's one within, who, having heard afar
Thy strange adventures in this seaside town, —
Thy loves, thy titles, and thy masquerades,
And more especially thy fearful duel
In the wood, — instanter boarded cars at Cornville
To rescue and to succor thee in peril;
She 's here, — she waits, — and now she doth appear.

He opens a door and SUSAN *enters.*

WHETSTONE.

Susan!

SUSAN.

Hercules!

WHETSTONE.

Dear Susan!

SUSAN.

Dear Hercules! [*They embrace.*

WHETSTONE.

Oh, Susan!

SUSAN [*surveying him*].

Why, Hercules, how you've changed! I do declare! your clothes are full of wrinkles. How thin you've grown! you must have lost twenty pounds! I must make you, this very night, a cup of my elder-blossom tea; I've brought the blossoms with me [*taking package from pocket*]. Hercules, can it be that you would have forsaken your Susan?

WHETSTONE.

Why, Susan!

SUSAN.

I knew it could never be.

WHETSTONE [*petting her*].

That's right, Susan; we'll be married. Think of it, we'll be married, Susan!

The Merchant Prince.

[*Music.* POMPEY *and* HANNIBAL *open doors on veranda, showing dining-hall; and* POMPEY *announces that dinner is served.*

NORTHLAKE.

May you all be my guests! There's indoors spread a merry cap-sheaf to this mirthful wooing. Let all proceed within.

VIOLET [*presenting* IDEAL].

Uncle, my Ideal.

NORTHLAKE.

Violet, my niece, happy art thou who hast for real thy Ideal.

VIOLET [*persuasively*].

Good uncle, thou wilt not cut down the tree in the orchard?

NORTHLAKE.

Nay, 't will bear good fruit in good season.

VIOLET [*to the company*].

A philosophic uncle, and a kind one.

CURTAIN.

www.ingramcontent.com/pod-product-compliance
Lightning Source LLC
Chambersburg PA
CBHW020013030726
47500CB00002B/562